全方位
英文聽力速成

⊙ 陳 頎 著 ⊙

書泉出版社 印行

序 (Preface)

　　筆者教學與演說多年，最常聽到學生或聽眾詢問的問題就是：「為何有些英文單字與對話都『讀』得懂，但是卻『聽』不懂？」其實英文聽力能力的養成需要有兩個面向——即時間的累積與技巧的掌握。其中時間的部分是要靠自己的努力與付出，而技巧的部分就需要老師或是一本好書的指導。

　　《全方位英文聽力速成》是筆者集多年英文聽力教學經驗的精華，書中歸納了各種英文聽力的技巧，包括最令人困擾的相似音以及連音、省音、變音等複雜規則，並針對英式與美式的發音及語調作清楚完整的對比。此外，本書還提供會考、學測、全民英檢（GEPT）與多益（TOEIC）等英文聽力考試相關仿真且實用性的試題演練，可讓讀者在各種英文聽力的測驗中拿取高分。

　　最後，筆者要特別感謝家人們對我的關愛，父親勤勉的人生態度，母親耐心的包容呵護，是筆者教學與寫作持續二十年最大的原動力。在此也感謝書泉出版社所給予的協助，本書雖精心編校，但疏漏難免，尚請讀者們不吝賜教。

陳　碩

目錄 (Contents)

聽力技巧實力提升 (PART 1)

聽力的練習應該是「熟悉深入」與「廣泛略聽」的結合

　　所謂「熟悉深入」的聽力練習，是指盡量把聽力的內容聽得十分透徹。建議學習者找出適合的聽力練習光碟，按照應有的步驟進行聽力練習。首先，先聽大意，也就是先聽出一段文字或是對話的大意就好。第二遍時，便採取逐句聽的方式，將CD的速度作幾次的暫停，給自己一些思考的時間。第三遍時，則試著做筆記，將所聽到的字句作一些摘要筆記。再來，則檢查實際的文字內容，試著找出自己所遺漏或是誤解的地方，最好是可以看著文字再來朗誦一遍。最後從頭到尾的再聽一次。確定百分之百都聽懂後，再進行下一題的練習。

　　另外，就是「廣泛略聽」。聽力的考試常有廣播題或是新聞與氣象報導題。所以學習者在聽到機場、車站、百貨超市等地方有英文廣播時，不妨多注意一下。平常時讓自己聽英文電臺、看英文版的電影或影集，亦或是看CNN等新聞報導半小時左右，不論是否完全了解，在每天持之以恆的努力下，我們對英文發音以及語調的敏感度自然會累積而越來越好。

英文發音的規則與化學變化

你是否明明每個字都看得懂或聽得懂，但是當外籍人士唸一整句時或用較快的速度朗誦時就聽不懂了？這是因為英文是他們所熟悉的母語，人類對於自己熟悉的語言，能快速的敘述，因此也出現了一些為了「方便說」的語音簡易法則，以下我們會學到英文發音中的連音變音等音的轉化，懂得這些規則，就能推出原本唸的是什麼字，自然就能聽懂字與字的前後關係與一整句的意涵。接下來我們針對音的變音省音弱音等音的化學變化來做介紹。

■ 本章重點

- 變音
- 連音
- 省音
- 弱音
- 縮寫字發音、Glottal T 音、特殊不發音
- 英文句子的語調
- 美式發音與英式發音的差異性
- 英式與美式用字與用句的差異

英文發音的規則與化學變化

連音

英文句子的語調

弱音

變音

省音

英式與美式用字與用句的差異

美式發音與英式發音的差異性

縮寫字發音、Glottal T音、特殊不發音

● **變音** 1-01

　　英文字中有一些常見的子音，為了發音的方便，往往會形成無聲變有聲的情況，以下我們先把常見的無聲變有聲的子音整理出來。

1. 字母 P 的發音

　　字母P的發音應該是無聲子音[p]，但是為求有效省力的發音方式，往往會加重其發音，也就是會出現無聲變有聲[b]的音。尤其當子音夾在兩個母音中間時，若能跟隨母音發出有聲子音（也就是音的同化現象assimilation），那就方便朗讀了。

　　另外，兩個無聲子音相鄰，如[sp]，第二個子音也會變成有聲，即發出[sb]的音。我們以下面的單字來作例字，第一遍會先聽到沒有變音的情況，第二遍則會出現變音。

母音的同化	1. Staple 2. Paper 3. Diaper 4. Pepper 5. Upper
子音的強化	6. Spring 7. Spill 8. Speak 9. Space 10. Spicy

2. 字母 k, c, ck, ch 的發音

　　字母k, c, ck, ch 的發音經常為無聲子音[k]，但是為求有效省力的發音方式，往往會加重其發音，也就是會出現無聲變有聲[g]的音。尤其當子音夾在兩個母音中間時，若能跟隨母音發出有聲子音，

那就方便朗讀了。另外，兩個無聲子音相鄰，如[sk]，第二個子音也會變成有聲，即發出[sg]的音。我們以下面的單字來作例字，第一遍會先聽到沒有變音的情況，第二遍則會出現變音。

母音的同化	1. Checkout
	2. Second
	3. Orchestra
	4. Package
	5. Weekend
子音的強化	6. Skill
	7. Skirt
	8. School
	9. Schedule
	10. Skip

3. 字母 t 的發音

字母T的發音應該是無聲子音[t]，但是為求有效省力的發音方式，往往會加重其發音，尤其當子音夾在兩個母音中間時，若能跟隨母音發出有聲子音[d]的音，那就方便朗讀了。兩個無聲子音相鄰，如[st]，第二個子音也會變成有聲，即發出[sd]的音。另外，當有兩個 tt 同時出現時，美式發音也多出現[d]的發音。我們以下面的單字來作例字，第一遍會先聽到沒有變音的情況，第二遍則會出現變音。

母音的同化	1. Autumn
	2. Motive
	3. Waiter
	4. Postage
	5. Notice
	6. Not at all

子音的強化	7. Stone 8. Stine 9. Step 10. Steady 11. Stock 12. Stop
tt 音的強化	13. Bottle 14. Letter 15. Battle 16. Mitten 17. Kitten 18. Betty

● 連音 1-02

　　變音介紹完之後，我們來整理連音。我們時常會發現，明明是兩個熟悉的單字，但是英美人士唸出來好像變成一個新的單字，這就是連音所造成的結果。若是我們能把以下的連音概念弄清楚，之後就不會有明明看得懂或是有背過，卻有聽不懂的遺憾囉！ 以下連音我們分三類整理：

1. 連音之子音＋母音（Consonant＋Vowel）

相鄰的兩個字，若是第一個字的結尾是子音，而第二個字的字首是母音，則兩個字就可以連起來讀。我們以下面的英文片語來作例字，第一遍會先聽到沒有連音的情況，第二遍則會唸出子音與母音的連結。例：

Get on	Call on	Turn on
Switch off	Put off	Take off
Pick up	Hold up	Line up
Find out	Call out	Give out
Believe in	Turn in	Get in
Take over	Turn over	Talk over
Right away	Put away	Throw away

以下的例句，我們會聽到一句不連音，一句連音的唸法：

 ▶ There are a lot of people in here.

　　 ▶ Let's have a cup of coffee.

　　 ▶ She is afraid of snakes.

　　 ▶ They see each other very often.

　　 ▶ I wish I were there.

　　 ▶ Stop it, will you?

　　 ▶ She left a week ago.

　　 ▶ The dog is barking.

　　 ▶ Shut up! Don't talk!

　　 ▶ The dress is expensive.

　　 ▶ Come on！ I don't believe you.

　　 ▶ Please say it aloud.

　　 ▶ Wait a second, are you kidding me?

　　 ▶ Most of us like that new comer.

　　 ▶ Did you hear it too?

2. 連音之母音＋母音（Vowel + Vowel）

　　相鄰的兩個字，若是第一個字的結尾是母音，而第二個字的開頭字首
又是母音，則為了幫助聲帶的顫動，可以在兩個字加一個過渡音來

作連結，常見的狀況為前面的母音為[i]，[ɪ]，[e]，[ə]，或是[aɪ]，則會衍生一個[j]的音出現；若前面的母音為[o]，[ɔ]或是[ʊ]，[u]，[aʊ]的音，則會衍生一個[w]的音。我們以下面的英文句子作範例，第一遍會先聽到沒有連音的狀況，第二遍則有連音的情況。

衍生[j]的音	1. Hurry up 2. May I have a pen? 3. Did you stay out last night? 4. See you later. 5. She ate three apples.
衍生[w]的音	6. How did you do it? 7. Do a little better. 8. She went into a big store. 9. You ought to study harder. 10. You may go or stay.

3. 連音與[j]相連之化學變化

此外，尚有一種我們稱作與[j]音相連會造成的化學變化，也就是念出一些比較特別的音。這類的狀況常見有四型：

[t]+[j]會變音成[tʃ]

[s]+[j]會變音成[ʃ]

[d]+[j]會變音成[dʒ]

[z]+[j]會變音成[ʒ]

而這類的情形會出現在一個單字中，或是字與字的連結中。

我們將每一個情形的例字舉出，而在例句的部分，我們第一遍會先聽到沒有化學變化的狀況，第二遍則有化學變化的情況。

◆ [t]+[j]會變音成[tʃ]

例字 picture/ nature/ future/ signature/ temperature/ moisture

例句 ▶ Nice to meet you!

▶ I hate you!

▶ Won't you give me a chance?

▶ Can't you make an exception?

▶ That's not your car.

◆ [s]+[j]會變音成[ʃ]

例字　issue/ tissue/ pressure/ sure/ assure/ insure

例句　▶ I want to kiss you!

▶ I miss you!

▶ I won't go abroad this year.

▶ I'll miss your family.

▶ I guess you're right!

◆ [d]+[j]會變音成[dʒ]

例字　educate/ residual/ individual/ graduate/ schedule/ procedure

例句　▶ Could you do me a favor?

▶ Would you say it again?

▶ Who returned your pens?

▶ Let me send you it.

▶ I need your help.

◆ [z]+[j]會變音成[ʒ]

例字　usually/ leisure/ pleasure/ measure/ visual / casual

例句　▶ Raise your hands.

▶ Close your book.

▶ How can I please you?

▶ Do not lose your ticket.

▶ As you please.

● 省音 1-03

　　兩字相鄰的英文字中，若前者的結尾是子音[p]，[b]，[t]，[d]，[k]，[g]等塞爆音，而後者的字首亦為子音時，兩字連讀為了發音的方便，第一個字的字尾往往會有被省略的情況。若前一字的結尾與後一字的開頭是同一個音時，前面的子音更會省略喔！

　　如公車站「bus stop」就不用唸兩次[s]的發音。以下的例字與例句，我們會先聽到沒有省略的情況，再聽到有省略的情況：

例字

▶ good morning

▶ good bye

▶ I don't know

▶ just there

▶ take care

▶ sit down

▶ some money

▶ you must go

▶ a good deal

▶ stop that

▶ last Saturday

▶ last night

▶ next Sunday

▶ next holiday

▶ you look great

▶ a big car

▶ a good girl

▶ blind date

▶ bus stop

▶ police station

▶ got to go

▶ please stop talking

▶ his sister

▶ concert ticket

▶ night market

例句 ▶ He has a big house.

▶ You look wonderful tonight.

▶ Did you take it back?

▶ You don't care, do you?

▶ What time did you arrive?

▶ Did you lock the door?

▶ We passed the TOEIC test.

▶ Please do it immediately.

▶ I will keep my word.

▶ Take care of yourselves.

● 弱音 1-04

　　英文的句子中有所謂重要的實字（content words），如一般的名詞與動詞等。這些字往往是這句話的重點，所以會凸顯來唸出。反之，有一些字是屬於功能詞（function words），如冠詞、人稱代

名詞、助動詞、be動詞、介系詞、連接詞或關係代名詞等，在句子中，所扮演的角色不重要，所以為求省力，其母音常被消弱。

1. 介系詞（Preposition）的弱化

常見的介系詞弱化有to, for, at, of, in 等。請聽以下的例句。

◆ **To 的例句**

例句 ▶ I work every day from eight to five. [tə]

▶ I look forward to your reply. [tə]

▶ She goes to school every morning. [tə]

▶ Tell me how to pronounce it. [tə]

▶ I have to go. [həftə]

▶ Mary has to study harder. [həstə]

▶ We are going to do it! [gonnə]

▶ I don't want to do it. [wɑnnə]

◆ **For 的例句**

例句 ▶ This award is for you. [fər]

▶ Thank you for saying so. [fər]

▶ It's time for lunch. [fər]

▶ Let's stop for the day. [fər]

▶ What do you eat for lunch? [fər]

◆ **At 例句**

例句 ▶ I finished my work at 10:00PM. [ət]

▶ Who's at the door? [ət]

▶ We study at school. [ət]

　　▶ I never smoke at the door. [ət]

　　▶ I want to retire at the age of 55. [ət]

◆ **Of** 例句

 ▶ It's a piece of cake. [əv]

　　▶ What kind of fruit do you like? [əv]

　　▶ Give me a couple of hours. [əv]

　　▶ As a matter of fact, you're wrong. [əv]

　　▶ One of us is a teacher. [əv]

　　▶ That's very kind of you. [əv]

◆ **In** 例句

 ▶ I am about to leave in five minutes. [ən]

　　▶ I am in such a hurry. [ən]

　　▶ What's in your bag? [ən]

　　▶ Put it in your pocket. [ən]

　　▶ He died in the war. [ən]

2. 連接詞（**Conjuction**）的弱化

常見的連接詞弱化有and, or, but, as 等。請聽以下的例句。

◆ **And** 例句

 ▶ Wait and see. [ən]

　　▶ Rock and Roll. [ən]

　　▶ And so on. [ən]

▶ He's jumping up <u>and</u> down. [ən]

▶ He's going in <u>and</u> out. [ən]

◆ **Or** 例句

 ▶ Coffee <u>or</u> tea? [ər]

▶ Rain <u>or</u> shine? [ər]

▶ I never smoke <u>or</u> drink. [ər]

▶ It took me one hour <u>or</u> so. [ər]

▶ Believe it <u>or</u> not. [ər]

◆ **But** 與 **As** 例句

 ▶ I'm poor <u>but</u> happy. [bət]

▶ She's pretty <u>but</u> a little short. [bət]

▶ Run <u>as</u> I do. [əz]

▶ Do it <u>as</u> I showed you before. [əz]

▶ Please come here <u>as</u> soon <u>as</u> possible. [əz]

3. 助動詞與 be 動詞的弱化

常見的助動詞弱化有can, would, have, has 等。請聽以下的例句。

 ▶ I <u>have</u> been to China before. [əv]

▶ They should <u>have</u> done it last night. [əv]

▶ She <u>has</u> learned English for many years. [əs]

▶ I <u>can</u> do it. [kən]

▶ Friday <u>would</u> be better. [wəd]

▶ So <u>am</u> I. [əm]

▶ What <u>was</u> he reading? [wəs]

4. h, th 與 t 的消弱化

◆ 有三個人稱代名詞的受格，會有弱音的情形：

(1) him 的三段發音變化：
原本發[hɪm]的音＞之後母音弱化為[həm]＞之後h又出現消音[əm]。

(2) her 的三段發音變化：
原本發[hɝ]的音＞之後母音弱化為[hər]＞之後h又出現消音[ər]。

(3) them 的三段發音變化：
原本發[ðæm]的音＞之後母音弱化為[ðəm]＞之後h又出現消音[əm]。

請聽以下的例句。

例句 ▶ We like him very much. [əm]

▶ Give him a hand. [əm]

▶ I love her a lot. [ər]

▶ Please forgive her. [ər]

▶ I hate them. [əm]

▶ Let them go. [əm]

◆ 人稱代名詞的主格「he」與所有格「his」，會有 h 消音的情形：

(1) he 的二段發音變化：
原本發[hi]的音＞之後h出現消音則變為變為[i]的音。

(2) his 的二段發音變化：
原本發[hɪz]的音＞之後h出現消音則變為變為[ɪz]的音。

請聽以下的例句。

例句 ▶ What's he doing? [i]

▶ Is he your father? [i]

▶ Does he work out every day? [i]

▶ Has he seen you before? [i]

▶ Where is he? [i]

▶ How does he work? [i]

▶ He lost his card. [ɪz]

▶ That's his watch. [ɪz]

● 縮寫字的發音，Glottal T 音與特殊不發音的情況 1-05

英文字在很多情況下會有縮寫字發音，Glottal T[tən]的發音以及特殊不發音的情況，我們也應該對這三種特殊情形的發音多加注意，如此對於聽力能力的提升，將有絕對的幫助。

1. 縮寫字發音練習

請聽以下的例句。

例句 ▶ I mayn't come.

▶ You can't do it.

▶ It couldn't be true.

▶ You mustn't tell anyone.

▶ You daren't say it, dare you?

▶ We didn't buy anything.

▶ I don't know the answer.

▶ She doesn't speak French.

- ▶ They <u>won't</u> be back until six.

- ▶ You <u>shouldn't</u> do things like that.

- ▶ She <u>isn't</u> coming to class.

- ▶ We <u>aren't</u> at home.

- ▶ Mary <u>wasn't</u> studying at that time.

- ▶ They <u>weren't</u> playing baseball then.

- ▶ He <u>hasn't</u> made up his mind.

- ▶ I <u>haven't</u> seen him for a long time.

- ▶ They <u>hadn't</u> found the lost key.

- ▶ You <u>needn't</u> give me a gift.

- ▶ She <u>wouldn't</u> tell her name.

- ▶ <u>I'm</u> happy.

- ▶ <u>You're</u> right.

- ▶ <u>He's</u> doing well.

- ▶ <u>She's</u> cute.

- ▶ <u>It's</u> mine.

- ▶ <u>We're</u> tall.

- ▶ <u>They're</u> heavy.

- ▶ <u>I'll</u> see you tomorrow.

- ▶ <u>She'll</u> try her best.

- ▶ <u>You'll</u> be sorry.

- ▶ <u>He'll</u> be right back.

- ▶ <u>It'll</u> be fine tomorrow.

- ▶ <u>That'll</u> be dangerous.

- ▶ <u>They'll</u> come next year.

▶ We'll be good.

▶ I've done it already.

▶ I'd be happy to.

▶ Let's dance.

▶ Here's your change.

▶ There's nothing to say.

▶ What's the matter with you?

2. Glottal T 發音練習

以下的例句，我們第一遍會先聽到代表字，第二遍則會聽到一整句。

 ▶ certain

I'm quite certain. 我十分確定。

▶ curtain

These are nice curtains. 這些是很棒的窗簾。

▶ cotton

It's 99% cotton. 它是99%棉質的。

▶ beaten

He is beaten. 他被打敗了。

▶ fountain

There's a water fountain. 有一個噴水池在那裡。

▶ written

The book is written in English. 這本書是用英文寫成的。

▶ button

Don't touch that button. 不要碰那個按鈕。

▶ threaten

Don't threaten me. 不要威脅我。

▶ Manhattan

Manhattan is a nice place. 曼哈頓是個好地方。

▶ mountain

Let's go mountain climbing. 讓我們去爬山。

▶ frighten

They are frightened. 他們很驚恐。

▶ bitten

I was bitten by a mean dog. 我被一隻惡狗咬。

3. 特殊不發音練習

特殊不發音有下列的狀況,並請聽例字:

gh 不發音	k 不發音	w 不發音	h 不發音	g 不發音	b 不發音	b 不發音
gh[x]	kn[n]	wr[r]	h[x]	gn[n]	bt[t]	mb[m]
Caught	Knife	Write	Honest	Gnaw	Debt	Bomb
Fought	Know	Wrong	Ghost	Gnat	Doubt	Dumb
High	Knee	Wrap	Hour	Gnash		Lamb
Right	Knack	Wreak				Thumb
Light	Knock	Wrote				Comb

● 英文句子的語調 1-06

在本章最後一節中,我們將討論英文句子中語調的概念。以下列舉三種形式的語調例句來作比較。

1. 降調：用於直述句、祈使句、wh問句

◆ 直述句

例句 ▶ You don't have a puppy.

▶ You shouldn't do things like that.

◆ 祈使句

例句 ▶ Please go there.

▶ Give me a break.

◆ wh 問句

例句 ▶ What is your address?

▶ Who has been to Germany?

▶ Why are they here?

▶ What happened to you?

2. 升調：一般是在問句的最後一個字語調才上揚，用於Yes-No問句

◆ YES-NO問句

例句 ▶ Will you see me next year?

▶ Can I have your last name?

3. 先升後降

◆ 選擇性的問句

(例句) ▶ Would you prefer tea or coffee?

▶ Was it sunny or windy?

◆ 系列句

(例句) ▶ The house has a kitchen, a bathroom, and a living room.

▶ She likes cats, dogs, and monkeys.

● 美式發音與英式發音的差異性 1-07

　　目前在臺灣的英文教育中，多強調標準的美式發音，美式發音好比是字正腔圓的國語，然而在一般的現實生活中，我們所遇到的絕對不是僅有美國人而已，所以往往聽力不錯的人，在遇到英式英語的發音或是澳洲腔時，就又出現鴨子聽雷的窘境。在各英語系的國家中，加拿大因為與美國地域相近，所以與美式腔調類似，而澳洲過去為英國的殖民地，所以澳洲腔與英國腔類似。其中，英式的發音因為母音發音較短，音調也較硬較重，往往對母語非英文的我們，形成一項較為嚴厲聽力的挑戰。但是為了能在職場上應對來自不同國家的人士，我們仍應該對各國的腔調都要有所了解。

　　以下我們列舉出美式與英式發音最大的幾個差異，並以例句與例字的方式，讓讀者作雙向的比較。

1. 母音 a 的差異

美式的母音a多發嘴巴裂大的扁音[æ]，在英式發音中，卻多為嘴巴張大[ɑ]的音，以下文例字與例句為例：

例字 apple/ aunt/ brass/ glass/ last/ after/class/ glance/ laugh/ bath/ pass/ path/ hast/mass

例句 ▶ Sally and Sam sat on a mat on Saturday.

▶ Frank got mad at his fat black cat.

▶ They danced on the grass last night.

▶ We laughed at Matt because he wore some stupid glasses.

▶ After taking a bath, I went to my class.

2. 母音 o 的差異

美式的母音o多發張大嘴巴的音[ɑ]，在英式發音中，卻多為嘴形較成圓形狀[ɔ]的音，以下文例字與例句為例：

例字 bog/ clock/ block/ flock/ hot/ fog/ cog/dot/ got/ soggy/ pop/ jog/ rob/ nod

例句 ▶ Drop me at the next block.

▶ We jog with Bob and his dog in the hot weather.

▶ I got some clocks and bottles in the grocery store.

▶ A pack of foxes disappeared when the fog came.

▶ Robbers in this robbery were arrested immediately.

3. 母音 u 的差異

美式的母音u發嘴型較呈尖形的音[u]，在英式發音中，卻多為嘴形較成圓形[ju]的音，即英文字「you」的發音，以下文例字與例句為例：

例字 blue/ flute/ nude/ tune/ clue/ glue/ rude/ cute/ June/super/ Luke/ flue/ supreme/ student

例句 ▶ A student named Luke is in the nude.

　　▶ I need some glue and a blue flute.

　　▶ They tune the instrument every June.

　　▶ The boy with a blue scarf is super cute.

　　▶ I have no clue why he is playing the flute in the nude.

4. 母音 er 與 air 的差異

美式的母音er 或是 air 都是捲舌音，er 發輕音[ə]或是重音[ɜ]，在英式發音中，er 與 air 則是發不強調捲舌的平音，如[ə]的音，以下文例字與例句爲例：

例字 air/ fair/ pair / her / herd / per / father / mother / sister / brother / teacher / fewer / later / wonder / wander

例句 ▶ My teacher Chad has short hair.

　　▶ My mother and father went to a popular fair.

　　▶ My brother and sister felt as if they were in the air.

　　▶ The farmer showed up at the fair later.

　　▶ My teacher worked so hard, and it's unfair he was fired.

5. 子音 tt 的差異

美式的tt音會加重成爲[d]音，在英式發音中，則是不發音，或是悶音，幾乎是聽不到的省略音，以下文例字與例句爲例：

例字 utter/ fatter/ bottle/ kitten/ butter/ bitter/ better/ pattern/ mitten/ matter/ letter/ battery/ quitter/ little

例句 ▶ This sentence pattern is better.

　　▶ No matter what happens, I am not a quitter.

▶ The <u>bottles</u>, <u>letters</u> and <u>batteries</u> are on the <u>little</u> table.

▶ I need some <u>butter</u>, not some <u>bitter</u> medicine.

▶ The <u>fattening kitten</u> is playing with the <u>mitten</u>.

● 英式與美式用字與用句的差異

　　美式與英式的英文，不但發音不同，就連在用字用句上，也有些許的不一樣。以下就列舉出美式英語以及英式英語最常見的用字上的不同。熟悉這些相異之處，對我們的聽力理解有絕對的幫助。

1. 英式與美式拼字

中文	美式	英式
中心	Center	Centre
支票	Check	Cheque
顏色	Color	Colour
榮譽	Honor	Honour
最愛的	Favorite	Favourite
勞工	Labor	Labour
珠寶	Jewelry	Jewellery
睡衣	Pajamas	Pyjamas
練習	Practice	Practise
了解	Realize	Realise
輪胎	Tire	Tyre
戲院	Theater	Theatre
公升	Liter	Litre
分析	Analyze	Analyse

中文	美式	英式
節目	Program	Programme
旅行者	Traveler	Traveller

2. 英式與美式用字

中文	美式	英式
公寓	Apartment	Flat
律師	Attorney, Lawyer	Barrister, Solicitor
飛機	Airplane	Aeroplane
罐	Can	Tin
糖果	Candy	Sweets
帳單	Check	Bill
餅乾	Cookie, Cracker	Biscuit
電梯	Elevator	Lift
水龍頭	Faucet	Tap
秋天	Fall	Autumn
一樓	First floor	Ground floor
二樓	Second floor	First floor
手電筒	Flashlight	Torch
薯條	French fries	Chips
忙線中	Busy on the phone	Engaged on the phone
垃圾	Garbage	Rubbish
汽油	Gas	Petrol
高速公路	Freeway	Motorway
十字路口	Intersection	Crossroads
郵件	Mail	Post

中文	美式	英式
電影	Movie	Film
電影院	Movie theater	Cinema
水壺	Pitcher	Jug
洋芋片	Chips	Crisps
鐵路	Railroad	Railway
廁所	Rest room	Public toilet
時刻表	Schedule	Timetable
人行道	Sidewalk	Pavement
球鞋	Sneakers	Sport shoes
排隊	In line	In queue
地鐵	Subway	Underground
卡車	Truck	Van
假期	Vacation	Holidays
擋風玻璃	Windshield	Windscreen

3. 英式與美式用句

中文	美式	英式
你有寵物嗎？	Do you have a pet?	Have you got a pet?
我要走了。	I have to go.	I've got to go.
我明天會見到你。	I will see you tomorrow.	I shall see you tomorrow.
他應該被告知是重要的。	It's imperative that he be told.	It's imperative that he should be told.
看起來快下雨了。	It looks like it is going to rain.	It looks as if it is going to rain.
（電話中）嗨，是Charles嗎？	Hello, is this Charles?	Hello, is that Charles?

中文	美式	英式
我的家人都很支持的。	My family is supportive.	My family are supportive.
一個人必須對自己負責。	One should take his own responsibility.	One should take one's own responsibility.

筆記頁

聽力的實力養成練習

在前一章我們學習到了英美人士發音與腔調的不同，以及英文句子中常見的連、變、省、弱的發音規則後，本書的第二章將以不同的方式來強化讀者的聽力能力的訓練，包括有日期與數字的練習，圖片的描述能力的練習，辨別問句的形式的練習，換句話說（in other words）的練習，聽力短文填空與改錯練習，以及聽力主題式詞彙，聽力同義字的掌握與聽力相似音的辨別，聽力同音異字與同字異音的辨別等。熟悉這一章的基礎練習後，接下來的實戰試題演練，就能輕輕鬆鬆地迎刃而解囉！

■ 本章重點

- 數字練習
- 圖片描述的能力
- 辨別問句不同形式的能力
- 換句話說的練習
- 聽力Q&A、填空、改錯的練習
- 聽力測驗方式的比較

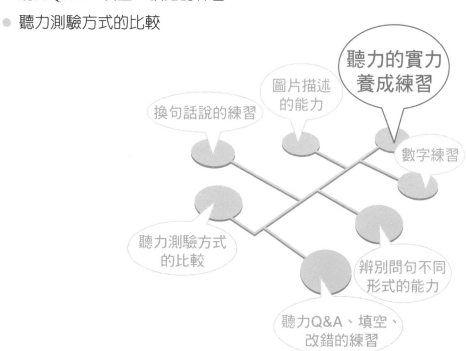

● 數字練習

以下我們針對不同的情形作練習：

比較數字的唸法：teen 發長音[i]，ty 的發音類似字母「D」的發音。			
13	thirteen	30	thirty
14	fourteen	40	forty
15	fifteen	50	fifty
16	sixteen	60	sixty
17	seventeen	70	seventy
18	eighteen	80	eighty
19	nineteen	90	ninety

一般百位與千位數字的唸法	
150	one hundred and fifty
624	six hundred and twenty-four
103	one hundred and three
965	nine hundred and sixty-five
5,298	five thousand, two hundred ninety-eight
6,373	six thousand, three hundred seventy-three
34,786	thirty-four thousand, seven hundred eighty-six
124,556	one hundred twenty-four thousand, five hundred fifty-six
1,416,922	one million, four hundred sixteen thousand, nine hundred twenty-two

電話號碼的唸法	
2378-3673	two three seven eight, three six seven three
6738-8903	six seven three eight, eight nine zero three
734-2233	seven three four, double two, double three
5673-2401	five six seven three, two four zero one
(07)689-7893 ext.303	Area code zero seven, six eight nine, seven eight nine three, extension three zero three

時間的唸法：

其中 quarter 是一刻鐘，也就是15分的意思；half 則是30分的意思。而「past」或「after」有「超過」的意思，如3:05，就是 five past/after three 三點過五分；而「to」或「before」則有「差」的意思，如2:55，就是 five to/before three 差五分就三點的意思。

5:15	five fifteen/ fifteen past five/ a quarter past five
7:47	seven forty-seven/ thirteen to eight
8:00	eight o'clock/ eight on the dot/ exactly eight
3:50	three fifty/ ten to four
9:30	nine thirty/ thirty to ten/ half to ten

分數的唸法：分子為基數 one, two, three 等，分母為序數 first, second, third 等，分子為 2 以上者，分母要加 s。

1/2	a half
1/3	one-third
1/4	one-fourth
3/4	three-fourths
2/5	two-fifths
4/7	four-sevenths
15/ 16	fifteen-sixteenths
1 and 1/2	one and a half

有數字地址的唸法：要兩位兩位數字來唸，不可以是單一的數字唸法，如167要唸成 one sixty-seven，不可以唸成 one six seven。

13 Maple Street	thirteen Maple Street
214 Park Avenue	two fourteen Park Avenue
2265 First Road	twenty-two sixty-five First Road
67483 Kennedy Boulevard	six seventy-four eighty-three Kennedy Boulevard

日期數字的唸法：日子須使用序數。	
January 2	January second
May 1	May first
August 8	August eighth
June 14	June fourteenth
December 25	December twenty-fifth

年代數字的唸法	
1916	nineteen sixteen
1017	ten seventeen
2006	two thousand and six
2011	two thousand eleven

● 圖片描述的能力

在平常的英文演練中，我們一定要培養看圖描述的習慣。圖片多為生活上隨手可得的東西，當我們見到一張圖片時，不妨用以下的角度來分析思考：

1. 這個（些）人的動作，以及他（們）作這個動作的目的。
2. 這些人的表情，體會圖片中人的喜怒哀樂。
3. 四周的環境與物品。
4. 個人對這張圖片的任何延伸想法。
5. 再用5W1H（What/Who/When/Where/Why/How）來思考一遍。

以下我們針對不同的圖片（分人物題與物件題）作練習，請用一句英文描述出所看見的圖片內容：

◆ 人物題

寫下所見的圖片內容

寫下所見的圖片內容

寫下所見的圖片內容

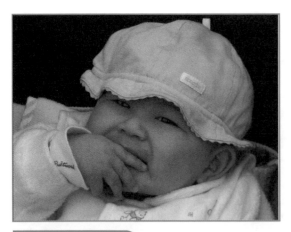

寫下所見的圖片內容

寫下所見的圖片內容

◆ 物件題

寫下所見的圖片內容

寫下所見的圖片內容

寫下所見的圖片內容

寫下所見的圖片內容

寫下所見的圖片內容

*參考答案請見 58 頁

● 辨別問句不同的形式的能力

在聽力的練習中，若要順利回應對方的問題，則必須對於問句的型態非常的熟悉，才能做正確的應答。如WH的問句不會回答YES與NO，Who's與Whose的不同等，都是學習英文聽力者要特別注意的地方。現行的一般聽力考試中，如英檢（GEPT）與多益（TOEIC）等，都有Question & Response的題型，因此辨別問句的不同形式，是聽力學習的一大重點。以下列舉在作這類 Question & Response 題型中，聽者常犯的一些錯誤：

1. 相似問句辨別錯誤

如What的問句中「What is the man?」是問這個人的職業，而「What is the man doing?」是問這個人正在做什麼？如 How的問句中「How does the man go to a movie?」是問這個人如何去看電影，要回應的應該是「交通模式」，而「How often does the man go to a movie?」是問這個人看電影的頻率，所以回應多為頻率副詞或是時間副詞。如在Who 的問句中「Who did the Mary see in the park?」是問Mary見到誰？而「Who saw Mary in the park?」是問誰見到Mary。在When 的問句中「When did the man leave?」是問這個人之前何時離開的，所以回應要為如last Friday（上週五）或five minutes ago（五分鐘前）等的過去的時間副詞；而「When will the man leave?」是問這個人將何時離去，所以回應要為如in 5 minutes（五分鐘後）或the day after tomorrow（後天）等未來的時間副詞。

2. 未聽清楚題目

▶ What is the man probably saying to the woman? 這男子可能對這女子說什麼？

► What is the woman probably saying to the man? 這女子可能對這男子說什麼？

3. 未聽清楚關鍵字

► He is <u>pouring</u> some coffee. 他正在「倒」咖啡。
► He is <u>drinking</u> some coffee. 他正在「喝」咖啡。
► He is <u>brewing</u> some coffee. 他正在「泡」咖啡。

4. 未聽清楚疑問詞

► <u>When</u> did your friend write the letter? 你的朋友「何時」寫這封信？
► <u>Where</u> did your friend write the letter? 你的朋友「在哪」寫這封信？

5. 未聽清楚慣用語

► Can you <u>give me a lift</u>? 可否載我一程？
► I am still <u>green on the job</u>. 我在這份工作上仍很生澀。

以下我們表格化問句的種類：

WH的問句
（5W+1H）

1. What/Which（什麼 / 哪一個）的問句

▶ What is the man talking about?
▶ What is the name of your company?
▶ What do you like to do in your leisure time?
▶ What is the purpose of your coming here?
▶ What are you going to do next year?
▶ What can your little sister do?
▶ What did you play in the room last night?
▶ What is your favorite subject at school?
▶ What is the time?=What time is it?
▶ What about going by taxi?
▶ What hotel in this city is the best?
▶ What is your refund policy on defective products?
▶ Which plan is easier to be carried out?
▶ Which one do you want, tea or coffee?

2. Who/Whose（誰 / 誰的）的問句

▶ Who comes here every day?
▶ Who wants to go the concert with me?
▶ Who is supposed to set up the conference room?
▶ Who will you meet tomorrow?
▶ Who is the best candidate you think?
▶ Who do you want to invite for Sunday's picnic?
▶ Whose car parked in front of the entrance?

★比較
Who's that? 那是誰？　回答爲：That is Charles.
Whose is that? 那是誰的？　回答爲：That is Charles's.

3. Why（為何）的問句

▶ Why is Nancy unhappy?
▶ Why did you do that?
▶ Why not go to a movie tonight?
▶ Why don't we meet together at a tea house?
▶ Why are you late?
▶ Why do you want to buy that sports car?
▶ Why is the year end appreciation dinner canceled?
▶ Why did he quit his good job?

4. When（何時）的問句

▶ When will they leave for the airport?

▶ When did they come here?

▶ When is the good time?

▶ When did you finish your presentation?

▶ When are you going to find out this?

▶ When did they graduate from college?

▶ When will you be back?

5. Where（在哪裡）的問句

▶ Where did you buy this pair of jeans?

▶ Where is the board meeting held?

▶ Where would you like to go for your vacation?

▶ Where is your place?

▶ Where are you from?

▶ Where can we sleep without paying too much?

▶ Where do the new students come from?

WH的問句
（5W+1H）

6. How（如何）的問句

▶ How do you want your steak?

▶ How did you know Mr. Charles Chen would be our new vice president?

▶ How do you do?

▶ How about watching flowers together?
(=What about watching flowers together?)

▶ How is the weather?
(=What is the weather like?)

▶ How are you doing? = How are you?

▶ How often do you take a computer class?（多常？）

▶ How far is it from here to your office?（多遠？）

▶ How old are your parents?（年紀多大？）

▶ How long have you been here?（多久？）

▶ How long ago did you start working here?（多久前？）

Yes-No問句

1. Be動詞開頭的問句

▶ Are they new in HR Dept.?
▶ Are you doing your homework?
▶ Is your father a doctor?
▶ Is your teacher from the United States?
▶ Was he playing computer when you called last night?
▶ Were they watching TV at this time yesterday?

2. 助動詞開頭的問句

▶ Did she ask Miss Lin to photocopy the report?
▶ Do you want to have a cup of coffee?
▶ Does your teacher teach well?
▶ Can they wait a second in the reception room?
▶ Could I use your car?
▶ Will they come here on time?
▶ Would you please repeat it?
▶ Must I answer all questions on the test sheet?
▶ May I be excused for leaving early?
▶ Should I open the window for you?

Or選擇性問句

1. Be動詞或助動詞開頭的 Or 問句

▶ Are they the new sales reps or not?
▶ Is your brother a student or an office worker?
▶ Do you want coffee or tea?
▶ Does she like flowers or chocolate?
▶ Will he come back on Monday or on Tuesday?

2. 疑問詞開頭的Or問句

▶ What would you like to eat after this boring meeting, Chinese food or Japanese food?
▶ Who is right, John or Mary?
▶ When should we start, now or later?
▶ Which is lighter, a cat or a tiger?
▶ Which is more expensive, an air conditioner or a fan?

	1. 一般的附加問句
附加問句	▶ Our new supervisor is so ambitious, isn't he?
	▶ You like Taiwan, don't you?
	▶ They can hear so far away, can't they?
	▶ We are the best, aren't we?
	▶ Mary should work harder, shouldn't she?
	2. 特殊句型的附加問句
	▶ Open the door, will you?
	▶ Don't go away, will you?
	▶ Let's go shopping, shall we?
	▶ I am smart, am I not?

● 換句話說的練習

在敘述一件事情時，我們會有許多不同的表達方式，在英文的敘述中亦是如此。例如：當我們說「Mary mustn't stay here.」（瑪麗不可以待在這裡）時，其實也就是「Mary has to leave here.」（瑪麗必須要離開）的意思。又例如：「I placed the order one week ago.」（我一週前下的訂單），也就是「Seven days ago I put in the order.」（七天前我下了訂單）。目前各英檢、留學英文聽力考試，多考考生聽（耳朵）與讀（眼睛）的轉換力，因此，多熟悉換句話說（In other words）的練習，對於聽力考試會有很大的幫助。

◆ 10句常見的「換句話說」

例句 ▶ Welcome to our <u>annual</u> luncheon party.
= The luncheon party is held <u>every year</u>.
歡迎來到我們每年一度的午餐會。
＝這午餐會每年辦一次。

▶ The weekend sale ends on Sunday.

 = The sale is on Saturday and Sunday.

 週末的特賣持續到週日。

 = 這個特賣週六與週日舉辦。

▶ I was too tired to go to work today.

 = I didn't go to work today.

 我今天太累以至於沒去上班。

 = 我今天沒有上班。

▶ Tom has been sitting in the classroom for two hours.

 = Tom is still sitting in the classroom now.

 湯姆在教室裡坐了兩小時。

 = 湯姆仍正坐在教室裡。

▶ We are understaffed now.

 = We need more staff now.

 我們人手不足。

 = 我們需要更多的員工。

▶ She'd like to see a movie.

 = She wants to see a movie.

 她想要去看電影

▶ The lesson is easy for Mary to do.

 = Mary does the lesson easily.

 這一課對瑪麗而言很容易。

▶ Susan called on her teacher yesterday.

 = Susan visited her teacher yesterday.

 蘇珊昨天拜訪她的老師。

▶ The baseball game has been called off.

 = The baseball game has been canceled.

 棒球賽已經取消了。

▶ We <u>deter that question</u> now.

= We <u>don't answer that question</u> now.

我們現在暫不回答那個問題。

◆ 以下請聽CD完成下列「換句話說」15題選擇題（圈出與所聽到的句子的同義句）2-01：

1. _____

    (A) The teacher probably got through the course.

    (B) The teacher probably didn't get through the course.

    (C) The teacher wanted me to get through the course.

2. _____

    (A) Jim called on his aunt.

    (B) Jim didn't call on his aunt.

    (C) Jim didn't study.

3. _____

    (A) He has been seeking for his cat for 60 minutes.

    (B) He is still looking for his cat.

    (C) He found his cat already.

4. _____

    (A) They never go to the lab.

    (B) They used to go to the lab.

    (C) They are used to going to the lab.

5. _____

    (A) Jane was frightening.

    (B) The movie was a funny one.

    (C) Jane was frightened.

6. _____

    (A) Peter didn't go to the library.

    (B) Peter swam before he went to the library.

    (C) John didn't go to the library.

7. _____

    (A) Betty didn't leave.

    (B) Bob left the house after Betty did.

    (C) Bob left the house before Betty did.

8. _____

    (A) Helen went to the university.

    (B) Nancy went to the graduate school.

    (C) Nancy didn't want to see Helen.

9. _____

    (A) I have two dresses.

    (B) I have four dresses.

    (C) I don't like green ones.

10. _____

    (A) Both Bill and Frank are going to give a speech.

    (B) Either Bill or Frank is going to give a speech.

    (C) Neither Bill nor Frank is going to give a speech.

11. _____

    (A) John is the tallest of three.

    (B) Jean is the tallest of three.

    (C) Mary is the tallest of three.

12. _____

(A) Susan telephoned her teacher two days ago.

(B) Susan visited her teacher two days ago.

(C) Susan telephoned her teacher yesterday.

13. _____

(A) Helen wants to go to class.

(B) Helen has a twin daughter.

(C) Helen's sister goes to class for Helen.

14. _____

(A) I read English magazines.

(B) I learned English and French.

(C) English magazines are expensive.

15. _____

(A) We don't pass the test.

(B) The teacher thought we could pass the test.

(C) The teacher gave a hard test.

*換句話說練習解答請見第 58 頁。

● 聽力Q&A、填空、改錯的練習

在一般的聽力考試中，有關於短文理解的聽力是考生最難拿分，也是最頭痛的部分。然而只要是英文的考試，留學考試如托福（TOEFL）與雅思（IELTS）與SAT，證照考試如多益（TOEIC）與全民英檢（GEPT），都會有短文（TALK）的考題。所以以下的這個章節我們將來練習許多的短文，由淺入深，將段落中的聽力關鍵字擬出，並藉由聽力填空與改錯的雙向練習，提升我們讀者的短文聽解能力。另外，為了在Q&A問答的題型上獲得高分，我們也應多進行一些Q&A的配對練習，以下就提供讀者三種的聽力實力養成的練習。

◆ 第一類練習（10題）：問與答（Q&A）的配對題

1. You won't believe what I heard today.

2. What are you looking for, ma'am?

3. Who's going to replace the marketing manager?

4. When did you get in?

5. Are you ready for tomorrow's presentation?

6. How would you like to send this package?

7. What dessert do you recommend?

8. Who's calling, please?

9. Can you make it to Tina's party tonight?

10. What made you so late?

- -

a. Let's wait and see.

b. Come on! Don't beat around the bush.

c. I ran into my old classmate on the way here.

d. I'm just looking.

e. Express, please.

f. I wish I could.

g. Just a little before Charles did.

h. No, thank you. I think I will work overtime today.

i. This is Charles Chen calling from AAA company.

j. All of them are good, I think.

請將答案填入以下空格

1	6
2	7
3	8
4	9
5	10

*問與答Q&A配對題解答請見第 61 頁。

◆ 第二類練習（10題）：短文聽力填空題

以下請聽CD完成短文聽力填充 2-02

短文一：請將下列的字填入文章中

fun fair   **charity party**   **community**   **Hope Foundation**   **give a speech**

Our _____ will hold a _____ in the town plaza next Saturday. We'll invite the head of _____ , Ms. Chen, to _____ about life and learning. In addition, there'll be a _____ , where you can enjoy a variety of different foods and different games.

短文二：請將下列的字填入文章中

did so well   **played**   **baseball**   **come with**   **next game**

Hi, Leo, this is Vincent. I'm really excited. I watched the _____ game yesterday and the Roxs _____ ! Wang _____ really well.He's really awesome! The _____ will be next week. Do you want to _____ me? Call me on my cell phone.

短文三：請將下列的字填入文章中

five   cashier   Department Store   patronage   items

Good evening, ladies and gentlemen. Thank you very much for visiting ABC _____ . We'll be closing in _____ minutes. Be sure to bring all the _____ you wish to purchase to the _____ . Thank you for shopping at ABC. Please visit us again, and many thanks for your _____ .

短文四：請將下列的字填入文章中

roller coaster   noted   Amusement Park   perfect place   eight

Welcome to Happy _____ . We have the most famous _____ in America, which is _____ for its exciting speed. For a magical night, just look up into the sky and enjoy the wonderful fireworks every night at _____ o'clock! Happy is the _____ for you and your family. And we can make you happy!

短文五：請將下列的字填入文章中

plane   Captain   be aware of   journey   attention to

This is _____ Andy speaking. We appreciate your full _____ the following announcement. This _____ has four emergency exits: two in the front of the plane and two in the back. Please _____ the exit near you. We hope you enjoy your _____ . Thank you so much.

短文六：請將下列的字填入文章中

overtime　**make it**　**cooking**　**some months**　**dinner**

Are you _____ now, Helen? My parents called to ask us to come home for _____ . Do you have to work _____ today? I think we should go to their place because we haven't seen them for _____ ____ and I kind of miss them. Let me know if you can _____ . Wait for your phone call. Bye!

短文七：請將下列的字填入文章中

be able to　**two months ago**　**Burger King**　**see a vet**　**kitten**

Hi, Mike. This is Ken. I won't _____ meet you at _____ this evening. That's because my _____ which was born _____ , suddenly got sick. I have to take her to _____ immediately. I am so sorry for that. I'll call you back soon. Talk to you later!

短文八：請將下列的字填入文章中

three articles of　**all the items**　**Department Store**　**half price**　**$3,000**

The Sears _____ is holding a special sale. In the women's wear department, if you buy _____ clothing, you get one free. And _____ in the Cosmetics department are under _____ . Additionally, most items in the accessories department are _____ . Ladies, you can't miss it!

短文九：請將下列的字填入文章中

promotion　$ 30,000　office　a three-day trip　20ᵗʰ anniversary

Attention all customers! To celebrate our _____ , we are having a special _____ today. If you spend _____ or more on office furniture, you can enter a drawing to win _____ to Japan. Take this great opportunity to redecorate your _____ and win this wonderful vacation!

短文十：請將下列的字填入文章中

stuff　tutor　small house　writer　composition

Hi, my name is Lucy. I live in a _____ with my grandparents in Taichung. I have a big bedroom. My grandmother puts a lot of _____ in my bedroom. I also have a study room where my _____ teaches me how to write good English _____ . I practice hard in that room every day. I hope I can be a good English _____ when I grow up!

*短文聽力填空題解答請見第 62 頁。

◆ 第三類練習（10題）：短文聽力改錯題

　以下請聽CD找出聽到與讀到的相異處 2-03

短文一：改正文章中的字句（共5個錯誤）

1 (　　)　2 (　　)　3 (　　)　4 (　　)　5 (　　)

Good morning, everyone! I am John. I live in Tainan with my grandparents. I share a bedroom with my older sister, Sara, but we don't have to share the bed. We don't have to share desks either. Sometimes, I enjoy doing housework or playing cards with my sister in our bedroom. But when I want to be alone in the room, I ask my sister to play or watch TV in the dining room. That's good.

短文二：改正文章中的字句（共5個錯誤）

1 (　　) 2 (　　) 3 (　　) 4 (　　) 5 (　　)

Hi, my name's Thomas Joes. I am a teacher at this school. I'm tall and I am twenty years old. Right now I live far away from the school, but I plan to move closer to the school some day. However, my friends say "no chance" because everybody wants to do the same thing. There aren't enough rooms for us.

短文三：改正文章中的字句（共5個錯誤）

1 (　　) 2 (　　) 3 (　　) 4 (　　) 5 (　　)

Hello, I'm Ted Anderson. I'm tall and handsome. I am not a new student at this school. This is my third year here. I am fifteen years old right now, but my birthday is tomorrow! So, I will be sixteen tomorrow. I live far from school and I always take the train to get here. To be honest, I am a little happy about taking a train. It takes me so long to contact.

短文四：改正文章中的字句（共5個錯誤）

1 (　　) 2 (　　) 3 (　　) 4 (　　) 5 (　　)

Hi everyone, my name is Max Chen. I am a third year student at this school and I live very far from here. I come from China and I am Chinese. My brother is a salesman here. I just turned 13 last year. English is my favorite subject. My father says I am an exceptional student in my class.

短文五：改正文章中的字句（共5個錯誤）

1（　　） 2（　　） 3（　　） 4（　　） 5（　　）

My name's Lily Archer and I am 30 years old. I am a new student at this university. I am Australian. I live very close to school. In fact, it only needs me one hour to get here! However, I am very happy I have to study English. I think English is a very hard subject.

短文六：改正文章中的字句（共5個錯誤）

1（　　） 2（　　） 3（　　） 4（　　） 5（　　）

I need you to help me make some changes to the schedule for my business trip next week. I'm going to have to take a night flight because my client wants to meet a day later than we had originally planned. If the flight is on Wednesday, I'll need an extra night booked at the motel there, too. And you know I always sit by the window, so don't give me an aisle seat please. After finishing everything, please connect me directly. Thanks so much.

短文七：改正文章中的字句（共5個錯誤）

1（　　） 2（　　） 3（　　） 4（　　） 5（　　）

Lisa was very busy today. First of all, she went to college. She took eight classes; in addition, she also did some part-time work at school. In class, she wrote and prescribed some important notes on paper. Later, she went to the library to find some books she needed. Nonetheless, she couldn't find them. What a shame! In the end, she gave up and went straight home. What a day it was.

短文八：改正文章中的字句（共5個錯誤）

1 (　　) 2 (　　) 3 (　　) 4 (　　) 5 (　　)

I try to do some exercises from time to time. Sometimes, I jog with my friends. Other times, I play basketball in the parking lot. My favorite sport of all is tennis. I play it with my family every weekend. Most of the time, I play in the front yard, but, once in a while, my partner and I play in the school. I think I love exercise, and I strongly believe that doing exercise is good and nice.

短文九：改正文章中的字句（共5個錯誤）

1 (　　) 2 (　　) 3 (　　) 4 (　　) 5 (　　)

English learners think that nouns are small but important words. They misplace nouns. Writers often use pronouns, so they won't have to repeat the same nouns over and over. Good readers look for pronouns when they read. They also look for the nouns that they infer to. This helps them read faster and understand more. Next time, when you study English, you should pay little attention to these small words.

短文十：改正文章中的字句（共5個錯誤）

1 (　　) 2 (　　) 3 (　　) 4 (　　) 5 (　　)

Good morning, everyone. Welcome to Taipei. I am your tourist, Gary. And this is Bill, our team leader. He is going to take us sightseeing at Taipei's most famous buildings for the following seven days. Right now, he is driving us to the second tallest building in the world, Taipei 101. You can visit the top of Taipei 101 or do some shopping in the hypermarket. Aslo, don't forgive some expositions in this skyline. It's about Taiwanese history. Enjoy it!

*短文聽力改錯題解答請見第 66 頁。

● 托福（TOEFL），雅思（IELTS），多益（TOEIC），英檢（GEPT），大學入學考試高中英語聽力測驗等考試方式的比較

　　以下說明留學考試（托福與雅思），英文證照考試（多益與英檢），以及大學入學考試聽力測驗題型比較：

托福 TOEFL	演講4-6篇，對話2-3段，測驗時間約60-90分鐘。其中4～6個演講，結合課堂討論，各3～5分鐘，包含6個問題。2～3個談話各3分鐘，包含5個問題。評分等級：0-30不同點。問題可以測出對說話者的態度、確實度、目的和動機的了解。可以做筆記。
雅思 IELTS	測驗時間30分鐘，分成四大主題，共40題，其中第一、二部分以生活語言為主，第三、四部分偏重學術性語言。以配對、是非、填充、選擇、簡答、標籤題等不同的答題方式。另有給予額外10分鐘讓考生將答案填寫於答案卡上。
新多益 NEW TOEIC	測驗時間為45分鐘，共100題，分其中題型為： 照片描述10題（一張圖片一題） 應答問題30題（一個問題三個選項） 簡短對話30題（共十組對話，每一組三題） 簡短獨白30題（共十組短文，每一組三題）

英檢 GEPT	初級聽力測驗	測驗項目	聽力測驗
		總題數	30題
		作答時間	約20分鐘
		測驗內容	看圖辨義、問答、簡短對話、短文聽解
	中級聽力測驗	測驗項目	聽力測驗
		總題數	45題
		作答時間	約30分鐘
		測驗內容	看圖辨義、問答、簡短對話
	中高級聽力測驗	測驗項目	聽力測驗

		總題數	45題
	中高級聽力測驗	作答時間	約35分鐘
		測驗內容	問答、簡短對話、簡短談話
英檢 GEPT		測驗項目	聽力測驗
		總題數	40題
	高級聽力測驗	作答時間	約45分鐘
		測驗內容	短篇對話及談話（Short Conversation and Talk）、長篇對話（Long Conversation）、長篇談話（Long Talk）
大學入學高中英語聽力測驗	測驗時間60分鐘（入場考試說明20分鐘，正式考試時間40分鐘），分成四大主題，每一大題各10題，共40題，分為看圖辨義、對答、簡短對話與短文聽解四類。（100年第一次試辦）		

*本書自第四章起，將有相關題目的演練喔！

■ 解答

◆ 人物題

圖一：People are discussing something in class.

圖二：There's a parade showing.

圖三：The man is writing on the whiteboard.

圖四：A cute baby is smiling.

圖五：People are walking across the street.

◆ 物件題

圖六：Delicious food is on the plate.

圖七：Books are arranged on the bookshelf.

圖八：All seats are vacant.

圖九：Boxes are stacked on the floor.

圖十：The road is lined with trees.

◆ 以下請聽CD完成下列「換句話說」15題選擇題：

1. I suppose that the teacher wanted me to finish the course.
   我想老師想要我完成這個課程。

   (A) The teacher probably got through the course.

   (B) The teacher probably didn't get through the course.

   (C) The teacher wanted me to get through the course.

   答案：(C) 老師要我完成這個課程。

   註：finish = get through 完成

2. Jim had planned to visit his aunt, but he had to study.
   吉姆原本計畫要去看他的阿姨，但是他必須讀書。

   (A) Jim called on his aunt.

   (B) Jim didn't call on his aunt.

   (C) Jim didn't study.

   答案：(B) 吉姆沒有去看他的阿姨。

   註：visit = call on 拜訪

3. He has been looking for his cat for half an hour.

    他持續找他的貓半小時了。

    (A) He has been seeking for his cat for 60 minutes.

    (B) He is still looking for his cat.

    (C) He found his cat already.

    答案：(B) 他仍然還在找他的貓。

    註：look for = seek 尋找

4. The students don't go to the lab anymore.

    學生們再也不去實驗室了。

    (A) They never go to the lab.

    (B) They used to go to the lab.

    (C) They are used to going to the lab.

    答案：(B) 他們以前去實驗室（現在不去了）。

    註：used to 過去曾經 / be used to 習慣於（兩者不同）

5. The movie frightened Jane.

    這部電影嚇到珍了。

    (A) Jane was frightening.

    (B) The movie was a funny one.

    (C) Jane was frightened.

    答案：(C) 珍感到很驚恐。

    註：frightening 令人驚嚇的 / frightened 感到驚嚇的

6. John went to the library while Peter was swimming.

    當約翰去圖書館時，彼得正在游泳。

    (A) Peter didn't go to the library.

    (B) Peter swam before he went to the library.

    (C) John didn't go to the library.

    答案：(A) 彼得沒去圖書館。

7. Bob left the house fifteen minutes ago. Betty left sooner than he did.

    鮑伯十五分鐘前離開家。貝蒂比他更早離開。

    (A) Betty didn't leave.

(B) Bob left the house after Betty did.

(C) Bob left the house before Betty did.

答案：(B) 鮑伯在貝蒂之後離開家。

8. Nancy hasn't seen Helen since she came to the university.

在海倫上大學後，南茜再也沒有見到她。

(A) Helen went to the university.

(B) Nancy went to the graduation school.

(C) Nancy didn't want to see Helen.

答案：(A) 海倫去上大學。

9. I have two green dresses and two yellow ones.

我有兩件綠色的洋裝與兩件黃色的洋裝。

(A) I have two dresses.

(B) I have four dresses.

(C) I don't like green ones.

答案：(B) 我有四件洋裝。

10. Bill is going to give a speech, and Frank is too.

比爾將要演說，而法蘭克也是。

(A) Both Bill and Frank are going to give a speech.

(B) Either Bill or Frank is going to give a speech.

(C) Neither Bill nor Frank is going to give a speech.

答案：(A) 比爾與法蘭克都要演說。

註：both...and... .（兩者皆是）/ either A or B（非A即B）/
neither A nor B（兩者皆非）

11. Jean is taller than John, but she is shorter than Mary.

珍比約翰高但比瑪麗矮。

(A) John is the tallest of three.

(B) Jean is the tallest of three.

(C) Mary is the tallest of three.

答案：(C) 瑪麗是三人中最高的。

12. Susan called up her teacher the day before yesterday.

蘇珊前天打電話給她的老師。

(A) **Susan telephoned her teacher two days ago.**

(B) Susan visited her teacher two days ago.

(C) Susan telephoned her teacher yesterday.

答案：(A) 蘇珊兩天前打電話給她的老師。

13. Helen gets her twin sister to go to class for her.

海倫要她的雙胞胎姊妹替她去上課。

(A) Helen wants to go to class.

(B) Helen has a twin daughter.

(C) **Helen's sister goes to class for Helen.**

答案：(C) 海倫的姊妹替海倫去上課。

14. I learn English by reading English magazines.

我藉由讀英文雜誌學英文。

(A) **I read English magazines.**

(B) I learned English and French.

(C) English magazines are expensive.

答案：(A) 我讀英文雜誌。

15. The teacher expected us to pass the test.

老師預期我們可以通過考試。

(A) We don't pass the test.

(B) **The teacher thought we could pass the test.**

(C) The teacher gave a hard test.

答案：(B) 老師認為我們可以通過考試。

◆ 第一類練習（10題）：Q&A的配對題

請將1-10的Q問與a-j的A答配對

1. You won't believe what I heard today.

   b. Come on! Don't beat around the bush.

2. What are you looking for, ma'am?

   d. I'm just looking.

3. Who's going to replace the Marketing manager?

   a. Let's wait and see.

4. When did you get in?

   g. Just a little before Charles did.

5. Are you ready for tomorrow's presentation?

   h. No, thank you. I think I will work overtime today.

6. How would you like to send this package?

   e. Express, please.

7. What dessert do you recommend?

   j. All of them are good, I think.

8. Who's calling, please?

   i. This is Charles Chen calling from AAA company.

9. Can you make it to Tina's party tonight?

   f. I wish I could.

10. What made you so late?

    c. I ran into my old classmate on the way here.

◆ 第二類練習（10題）：短文聽力填空題

短文一：請將下列的字填入文章中

fun fair　charity party　community　Hope Foundation　give a speech

Our **community** will hold a **charity party** in the town plaza next Saturday. We'll invite the head of **Hope Foundation**, Ms. Chen, to **give a speech** about life and learning. In addition, there'll be a **fun fair**, where you can enjoy a variety of different foods and different games.

短文二：請將下列的字填入文章中

did so well　played　baseball　come with　next game

Hi, Leo, this is Vincent. I'm really excited. I watched the **baseball** game yesterday and the Roxs **did so well**! Wang **played** really well. He's really awesome! The **next game** will be next week. Do you want to **come with** me? Call me on my cell phone.

短文三：請將下列的字填入文章中

five　cashier　Department Store　patronage　items

Good evening, ladies and gentlemen. Thank you very much for visiting ABC **Department Store**. We'll be closing in **five** minutes. Be sure to bring all the **items** you wish to purchase to the **cashier**. Thank you for shopping at ABC. Please visit us again, and many thanks for your **patronage**.

短文四：請將下列的字填入文章中

roller coaster　noted　Amusement Park　perfect place　eight

Welcome to Happy **Amusement Park**. We have the most famous **roller coaster** in America, which is **noted** for its exciting speed. For a magical night, just look up into the sky and enjoy the wonderful fireworks every night at **eight** o'clock! Happy is the **perfect place** for you and your family. And we can make you happy!

短文五：請將下列的字填入文章中

plane　Captain　be aware of　journey　attention to

This is **Captain** Andy speaking. We appreciate your full **attention to** the following announcement. This **plane** has four emergency exits: two in the front of the plane and two in the back. Please **be aware of** the exit near you. We hope you enjoy your **journey**. Thank you so much.

短文六：請將下列的字填入文章中

overtime　make it　cooking　some months　dinner

Are you **cooking** now, Helen? My parents called to ask us to come home for **dinner**. Do you have to work **overtime** today? I think we should go to their place because we haven't seen them for **some months** and I kind of miss them. Let me know if you can **make it**. Wait for your phone call. Bye!

短文七：請將下列的字填入文章中

be able to　two months ago　Burger King　see a vet　kitten

Hi, Mike. This is Ken. I won't **be able to** meet you at **Burger King** this evening, That's because my **kitten** which was born **two months ago**, suddenly got sick. I have to take her to **see a vet** immediately. I am som sorry for that. I'll call you back soon. Talk to you later!

短文八：請將下列的字填入文章中

three articles of　**all the items**　**Department Store**　**half price**　**$3,000**

The Sears **Department Store** is holding a special sale. In the women's wear department, if you buy **three articles of** clothing, you get one free. And **all the items** in the Cosmetics department are under **$3, 000**. Additionally, most items in the accessories department are **half price**. Ladies, you can't miss it!

短文九：請將下列的字填入文章中

promotion　**$ 30,000**　**office**　**a three-day trip**　**20th anniversary**

Attention all customers! To celebrate our **20th anniversary**, we are having a special **promotion** today. If you spend **$ 30, 000** or more on office furniture, you can enter a drawing to win **a three-day trip** to Japan. Take this great opportunity to redecorate your **office** and win this wonderful vacation!

短文十：請將下列的字填入文章中

stuff　**tutor**　**small house**　**writer**　**composition**

Hi, my name is Lucy. I live in a **small house** with my grandparents in Taichung. I have a big bedroom. My grandmother puts a lot of **stuff** in my bedroom. I also have a study room where my **tutor** teaches me how to write good English **composition**. I practice hard in that room every day. I hope I can be a good English **writer** when I grow up!

◆ 第三類練習（10題）：短文聽力改錯題

短文一：改正文章中的字句（共5個錯誤）

Good morning, everyone! I am John. I live in Tainan with my **parents**. I share a bedroom with my **younger** sister, Sara, but we don't have to share the bed. We don't have to share **closets** either. Sometimes, I enjoy doing **homework** or playing cards with my sister in our bedroom. But when I want to be alone in the room, I ask my sister to play or watch TV in the **living room**. That's good.

短文二：改正文章中的字句（共5個錯誤）

Hi, my name's Thomas Joes. I am a **student** at this school. I'm **short** and I am **twelve** years old. Right now I live far away from the school, but I plan to move closer to the school some day. However, my friends say "**fat** chance" because everybody wants to do the same thing. There aren't enough **places** for us.

短文三：改正文章中的字句（共5個錯誤）

Hello, I'm Ted Anderson. I'm tall and handsome. I am not a new student at this school. This is my **second** year here. I am **fourteen** years old right now, but my birthday is tomorrow! So, I will be **fifteen** tomorrow. I live far from school and I always take the train to get here. To be honest, I am a little **tired of** taking a train. It takes me so long to **commute**.

短文四：改正文章中的字句（共5個錯誤）

Hi everyone, my name is Max Chen. I am a **second** year student at this school and I live very **near** here. I come from China and I am Chinese. My brother is a **businessman** here. I just turned **12** last year. English is my favorite subject. My **teacher** says I am an exceptional student in my class.

短文五： 改正文章中的字句（共5個錯誤）

My name's Lily Archer and I am 30 years old. I am a new student at this **college**. I am **African**. I live very close to school. In fact, it only **takes** me one hour to get here! However, I am very **upset** I have to study English. I think English is a very hard **language**.

短文六： 改正文章中的字句（共5個錯誤）

I need you to help me make some changes to the **itinerary** for my business trip next week. I'm going to have to take a **late** flight because my client wants to meet a day later than we had originally planned. If the flight is on **Monday**, I'll need an extra night booked at the **hotel** there, too. And you know I always sit by the window, so don't give me an aisle seat please. After finishing everything, please **contact** me directly. Thanks so much.

短文七： 改正文章中的字句（共5個錯誤）

Lisa was very busy today. First of all, she went to **school**. She took eight classes; **additionally**, she also did some part-time work at school. In class, she wrote and **transcribed** some important notes on paper. Later, she went to the library to find some books she needed. **However**, she couldn't find them. What a shame! **Finally**, she gave up and went straight home. What a day it was.

短文八： 改正文章中的字句（共5個錯誤）

I try to do some exercises **all the time**. Sometimes, I jog with my friends. Other times, I play basketball in the **park**. My favorite sport of all is tennis. I play it with my family every weekend. Most of the time, I play in the **courtyard**, but, once in a while, my partner and I play in the **gym**. I think I love exercise, and I strongly believe that doing exercise is good and **beneficial**.

短文九： 改正文章中的字句（共5個錯誤）

English learners think that **pronouns** are small but important words. They **replace** nouns. Writers often use pronouns, so they won't have to repeat the same nouns **again and again**. Good readers look for pronouns when they read. They also look for the nouns that they **refer** to. This helps them read faster and understand more. Next time, when you study English, you should pay **more** attention to these small words.

短文十： 改正文章中的字句（共5個錯誤）

Good morning, everyone. Welcome to Taipei. I am your **tour guide**, Gary. And this is Bill, our team leader. He is going to take us sightseeing at Taipei's most famous **parks** for the following seven days. Right now, he is driving us to the second tallest building in the world, Taipei 101.You can visit the top of Taipei 101 or do some shopping in the **department store**. Aslo, don't forget some **exhibitions** in this **skyscraper**. It's about Taiwanese history. Enjoy it!

聽力字彙的掌握

有關聽力字彙的學習，可以由以下幾個不同的層次來探討學習。第一個部分就屬於「主題字彙的掌握」，如與機場和飛機有關的字彙有：concourse（機場大廳），airline ticket counter（航空公司櫃檯），courtesy desk（服務臺），baggage claim area（行李認領處），gate（登機門），overhead compartment（飛機上的置物櫃）等。我們若能掌握並熟悉這些單字，當我們聽到這些字時，就能知道這是機場內或是飛機上的對話或是獨白，這樣對於聽力理解的流暢度就會有所幫助。

在平常的練習中，我們也可以利用連結圖（Semantic Map）的方式，來聯想相關的主題字彙，如此對於我們的聽力單字養成，就會有絕對的幫助：

連結圖（Semantic Map）範例：

■本章重點

● 分類主題式聽力字彙

● 聽力題中同義字彙的掌握

● 相似音，同音異字或同字異音，多重含意字

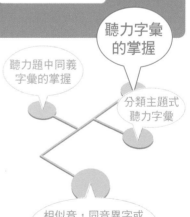

● 分類主題式聽力字彙

　　以下我們挑選針對不同的主題（共二十種大類），以及高頻率出現的單字，來作聽力場景字彙的分類整理。

◆ 機場或在飛機上用字

英文	中文
Information booth	詢問臺
Terminal	航站大廈
Waiting area	候機室
Duty-free shop	免稅商店
Security checkpoint	安檢關卡
Declaration form	申報單
Customs	海關
Customs officer	海關人員
Passenger	旅客
Nose	機頭
Cabin	機艙
Tail	機尾
Aisle seat	靠走道座位
Window seat	靠窗座位
Air sickness	暈機
Suitcase / Briefcase	行李
Timetable	時刻表
Ticket counter	售票處
Runway	跑道
Gate	登機門
Boarding pass	登機證

英文	中文
Immigration	出入境檢查
Passport	護照
Flight attendant	空服員
Oxygen mask	氧氣罩
Lavatory	廁所
Baggage claim	行李認領處
Baggage carousel	旋轉式行李輸送帶
Carry-on item	手提行李
Overhead compartment / Overhead bins	飛機座位上方置物櫃
Captain	機長
Jet lag	時差

◆ 自然環境用字

英文	中文
Forest	森林
Woods	樹林
Meadow	草地
Plain	平原
Plateau	高原
Valley	山谷
Hill	山丘
Stream	溪流
River	河川
Desert	沙漠
Oasis	綠洲

英文	中文
Mirage	海市蜃樓
Lake	湖
Pond	池塘
Waterfall	瀑布
Field	農田
Canyon	峽谷
Dam	水壩
Jungle	叢林
Seashore	海岸
Beach	海灘
Iceberg	冰山
Glacier	冰河
Bay	海灣
Island	島嶼
Islet	小島
Continent	洲
Mainland	大陸
Wading pool	淺水池
Grass	草皮
Volcano	火山
Bush	矮木叢

◆ 教育人員用字

英文	中文
Founder	創辦人
Promoter	發起人

英文	中文
President / Chancellor	大學校長
Principal	中學校長
Master	小學校長
Commandant	軍校校長
Dean	院長
Department head	系主任
Professor	教授
Advisor	指導教授
Emeritus Professor	榮譽教授
Visiting Professor	客座教授
Associate Professor	副教授
Assistance Professor	助理教授
Lecturer / Instructor	講師
Assistant	助教

◆ 醫學用字

英文	中文
Doctor	醫師
Dentist	牙醫
Physician	內科醫生
Surgeon	外科醫生
Vet	獸醫
Pediatrician	小兒科醫生
Psychiatrist	精神科醫生
Cardiologist	心臟科醫師
Lab technician	化驗員

英文	中文
Oral hygienist	洗牙師
Optometrist	驗光醫師
Gynecologist	婦科醫師
Stethoscope	聽診器
Gloves	醫療手套
Syringe	針筒
Needle	針頭
Alcohol	酒精
Drill	牙鑽
Eye chart	視力表
Thermometer	體溫計
Blood pressure gauge	血壓計
Gauze	紗布
Cotton balls	棉球
Anesthetic	麻醉劑
Prescription	處方
Stitches	傷口縫針
Surgery	動手術
Injection	注射
Cast	石膏
Blood tests	驗血
Counseling	心理治療
Bandage	繃帶

◆ 辦公室用品用字

英文	中文
Employee lounge	員工休息室
Workbench	工作臺
Meeting room / Conference room	會議室
Keyboard	鍵盤
Monitor	螢幕
Reception area	接待室
Supply room	用品室
Word processor	文字處理系統
Facsimile / Fax machine	傳真機
Pencil shredder	削鉛筆機
Stationery	辦公文具
Presentation slides	投影片
File cabinet / File closet	檔案櫃
Marker	馬克筆
Desktop computer / Desktop	桌上型電腦
Printer	印表機
Overhead projector	投影機
Podium	講臺
Microphone	麥克風
Organizer	行事曆
Letter opener	拆信刀
Copying machine / Photocopier	影印機
Stapler	訂書機
Tape dispenser	膠臺座
Paper clip	迴紋針

英文	中文
Stamp pad	印泥
Carbon paper	複寫紙
Loudspeaker	擴音器
Handout	講義
Whiteboard	白板
Correction fluid	修正液
Rubber stamp	圖章
Post-it notes	便利貼
Paper cutter	裁紙機
Paper shredder	碎紙機
Swivel chair	旋轉椅
Blinds / Shutters	百葉窗
Stationery	文具
Supply cabinet	儲藏櫃
Employee lounge	員工休息室
Files	檔案

◆ 旅館用字

英文	中文
Valet parking	代客停車
Bellhop	行李小弟
Guest room	客房
Room service	客房用餐服務
Housekeeping cart	房間清理車
Ballroom	宴會廳
Doorman	門房

英文	中文
Bell captain	行李總管
Luggage cart	行李車
Housekeeper	清潔人員
Concierge	接待人員
Continental breakfast	歐式自助餐
President suite	總統套房
Twin room	兩小床的雙人房
Quadruple	四人房
Pay-per-view movie	付費電影
Limousine	禮車
Complimentary breakfast	免費早餐
Spa service	SPA服務
Massage service	按摩服務
Sauna	烤箱，三溫暖
Itinerary	預定行程
High-season charge	旺季費用
Operator	接線生
Steam room	蒸氣室
Jacuzzi	按摩池
Laundry service	洗衣服務
Off-season charge	淡季費用
Lounge bars	酒吧
Safety deposit box	保險箱
City guide	城市導覽
Package tour	套裝行程
Jacuzzi	按摩浴缸

英文	中文
Lounge bar	酒吧
Amusement park	遊樂園
Theme park	主題樂園
Resort	度假勝地
Tourist spots	觀光景點
Botanical garden	植物園
Statue	雕像
Monument	紀念碑
Sightseeing	觀光
Ocean view	海景

◆ 職場職稱用字

英文職稱	中文職稱	英文職稱	中文職稱
Chairman	董事長	President	總裁
Vice chairman	副董事長	Vice president	副總裁
Executive(CEO)	執行長	General manager	總經理
Director	主任	Vice general manager	副總經理
Vice director	副主任	Special assistant	特別助理
Manager	經理	Factory chief	廠長
Assistant manager	副理	Factory sub-chief	副廠長
Assistant manager	協理	Chief engineer	首席工程師
Junior manager	襄理	System engineer	系統工程師
Section manager	課長	Senior engineer	高級工程師
Deputy section manager	副課長	Engineer	工程師

英文職稱	中文職稱	英文職稱	中文職稱
Specialist	專員	Deputy engineer	副工程師
Administrator	管理師； 行政人員	Assistant engineer	助理工程師
Deputy administrator	副管理師	Managing technician	管理員
Supervisor	組長	Senior technician	高級技術員
Deputy supervisor	副組長	Technician	技術員
Representative (Rep)	代表	Team leader	領班
Secretary	祕書	Assistant technician	助理技術員
Staff	職員	Operator	作業員；總機
Assistant	助理	Receptionist	櫃檯人員
Clerk	事務員	Usher / Escort	引導（座）員
Senior clerk	組員	Chauffeur	私人司機

英文	中文
Global warming	全球暖化
Heat wave	熱浪
Huge floods	洪水
Gulf stream	墨西哥灣流
Melt ice	融冰
Weather phenomena	大氣現象
Coast water level	海平面
Devastating	毀滅性的
Polar ice caps	極地冰帽
Atmosphere	大氣層

英文	中文
Recycle	回收
Greenhouse effect	溫室效應
Carbon dioxide	二氧化碳
Industrial revolution	工業革命
Inter-government Panel on Climate Change (IPCC)	聯合國氣候變化跨國組織

◆ 天氣相關字彙

英文	中文
Precipitation	降雨量
Cloudburst	豪雨
Drench	滂沱大雨
Drizzle	毛毛雨
Sprinkle	稀疏小雨
Typhoon	颱風
Hurricane	颶風
Twister / Tornado	龍捲風
Thunderstorm	大雷雨
Gust	強風
Breeze	微風
Wind	風
Turbulence	亂流
Low pressure	低氣壓
High pressure	高氣壓
Temperature	氣溫
Drought / Aridity	乾旱

英文	中文
Flood / Inundation	洪水
Deluge	洪水暴雨

◆ 電腦科技相關字彙

英文	中文
Access	進入使用
Cutting edge	尖端
Digital	數位的
Download	下載
Hacker	駭客
Laptop	筆記型電腦
Multimedia	多媒體
Retrieval	取回
State-of-the-art	最新先進技術的
Terminology	專業術語
Troubleshooting	檢修（解決困難）
Activate	啓動
Browse	瀏覽
Database	資料庫
Hyperlink	超連結
Know-how	專業技能
Modem	數據機
Server	伺服器
Transmission	傳輸
Upgrade	升級
Virus	病毒

◆ 身體的病痛相關字彙

英文	中文
Ailment	病痛
Diarrhea	腹瀉
Flu	感冒
Constipation	便祕
Sore throat	喉嚨痛
Rash	出疹子
Indigestion	消化不良
Cuts	割傷
Sprained ankle	扭傷腳踝
High blood pressure	高血壓
Sleep deprivation	睡眠剝奪
Influenza	流感
Bronchitis	支氣管炎
Resistibility	抵抗力
Nausea	噁心
Symptom	症狀
Trauma	外傷
Hypersensitive	過敏症
Arthritis	關節炎
High cholesterol	高膽固醇

◆ 企業管理相關字彙

英文	中文
Media exposure	媒體曝光率
Door-to-door customer contact	與顧客面對面接觸

英文	中文
Technology management	科技管理
Business negotiations	商業談判
Accounting	會計學
Business essentials	企業概論
Economics	經濟學
Marketing	行銷學
Financial management	財務管理
Accounting management	帳務管理
Applied management	經營實務
Applied marketing and project management	行銷企劃實務
Brand management	品牌管理
Business communication	商用溝通技巧
Business diagnosis	企業診斷
Business law	商事法
Business policy	企業政策
E-commerce	電子商務
E-enterprises	電子化企業
E-marketing	網路行銷
Enterprise merger	企業併購
Future and options	期貨與選擇權
Human resource management	人力資源管理
Information management	資訊管理
International business management	國際企業管理
International enterprises	國際企業
International marketing	國際行銷

英文	中文
Investments	投資學
Macroeconomics	總體經濟學
Management accounting	管理會計
Managerial decision	管理決策
Marketing distribution management	行銷通路管理
Marketing in service industry	服務業行銷
Microeconomics	個體經濟學
Operational management	作業管理
Organization development and change	組織發展與變革管理
Organizational behavior	組織行為
Re-engineering of enterprises	企業再造
Small-and-medium scale enterprises management	中小企業管理
Statistics	統計學
Supply chain management	供應鏈管理
Taxation law	稅務法規

◆ 餐廳相關字彙

英文	中文
Restaurant	餐廳
Silverware	銀餐具
Server	服務人員
Waiter / Waitress	男（女）服務生
Diner	用餐者
Check / Bill	帳單
Chef / Cook	廚師

英文	中文
Cook / Cookware	煮飯的器具
Menu	菜單
A Table For Four	四人的座位
Patio	內院
Appetizer	開胃菜
Main dish / Main course / Antrée	主餐
Dessert	甜點
Beverage / Drink	飲料
Make a reservation	預約
Set the table	擺設桌子
Display the tood	展示食物
Buffet dinner	西式自助餐
Cook's specialty	廚師的拿手好菜
Tip	小費
Tasty / Delicious / Yummy	美味的
Ingredient	食材
Cookbook	食譜
Recipe	烹飪法
Overbooked	已經訂滿了
Stir-fry	快炒
Bus person	餐廳侍者
Grilled fish	烤魚
Stew	燉煮
Salad dressing	沙拉醬
Platter	大盤子
Tablecloth	桌布

英文	中文
Napkin	餐巾
Candlestick	燭臺
Salt / Pepper shaker	鹽 / 胡椒瓶
Butter knife	奶油刀
Serving cart	上餐的推車

◆ 與打球有關相關字彙

英文	中文
Serve	發球
Pitch	投球
Hit	打擊
Pass	傳球
Shoot	投射
Dribble / Bounce	運球
Kick	踢球
Tackle	攔截球
Dodge	躲避
Catch	接球
Throw	丟球

◆ 與國際貿易有關相關字彙

英文	中文
Trade surplus	貿易順差
Trade deficit	貿易逆差
Bilateral trade	雙邊貿易

英文	中文
Triangle sales	三角貿易
Monopoly	壟斷
Middleman	掮客
Distributor	經銷商
Free trade area	自由貿易區
Exchange rate fluctuation	浮動匯率
Rock bottom price	最低價
Ceiling price	最高價
Closing price	收盤價
Retail price	零售價
Mass production	大規模生產
Best seller	暢銷品
Poor seller	滯銷品
Payment in advance	預先付款
Upstream vendor	上游廠商
Downstream vendor	下游廠商
Competitive edge	競手優勢

◆ 與交通有關相關字彙

英文	中文
Route	路線
Platform	月臺
Transfer	轉車
Fare	車費
Track	軌道
Taxi stand	計程車招呼站

英文	中文
Pedestrian	行人
Conductor	車掌
Speed limit	速限
Timetable	時刻表
Express train	特快車
Railroad crossing	鐵路平交道

◆ 地震相關字彙

英文	中文
Earthquake (Quake)	地震
The trembling or shaking movement	震動與搖動
Buildings collapse	大樓坍塌
Vibration	震動
Epicenter	震央
Seismic waves	震波
Crust	地殼
Expansion and contraction	膨脹與收縮
Landslide and rockfall	山崩與落石
Earthquake intensity (magnitude)	地震強度
The richter scale	芮氏地震分等標準
Tsunami	海嘯
Seismograph	地震計
Seismologist	地震學家
Predictions of earthquake	地震預測
Trapped under the mountain of steel and concrete	受困於鋼筋水泥之下

英文	中文
Moan in pain	痛苦中呻吟
Rescue workers	救難隊員
Crush	擠壓
Tremor	顫動

◆ 洪水相關英文字彙

英文	中文
Inundation	洪水氾濫
Deluge	大洪水
Precipitation	降雨量
Flood	洪水
Overflow	氾濫
Low-lying area	低窪地區
Evacuation	撤離
Victim	受難者
Landslide	山崩，土石流
Contribution	捐獻
Donate food and clothing	貢獻食物與衣物
Reconstruction	重建

◆ 旅行相關英文字彙

英文	中文
Voyage	航行
Stopover	中途停留
Round-trip	來回的

英文	中文
Metal detector	金屬探測器
Exotic	異國風情的
Deluxe	豪華的
Cruise	乘船遊覽
Concierge	管理員
Carry-on	手提行李
Breathtaking	驚人的
Valid	有效期
Suite	旅館套房
Sightseeing	觀光
Peak Season	高峰期
Luxurious	奢侈的
Itinerary	行程表
Expedition	遠征隊
En route	在途中
Customs	海關
Departure	出發
Accommodation	住所

◆ 商業金融相關英文字彙

英文	中文
Amount in figures	小寫金額
Amount in words	大寫金額
Angel investor	散戶
Auction house	拍賣公司
Bank guarantee	銀行擔保

英文	中文
Bargain hunting	逢低買進
Beneficiary certificates	受益憑證
Board of directors	董事會
Bond market	債券市場
Bourse	證券交易所
Brand slut	對特定品牌沒有忠誠度的消費者
Business traveler	商務旅客
Cash flow	現金流
Certification	認證
Chief executive officer (CEO)	執行長
Chief financial officer (CFO)	財務長
Chindia	中印
Consumer durable goods	耐久消費財
Consumer non-durable goods	不耐久消費財
Consumer price index (CPI)	消費者指數
Corporate re-engineering	企業再造
Day trading	當日沖銷
Debt market	債務市場
Delivery date	交割日
Derivatives	衍生性金融商品
Discretionary account operation	代客操作
Distribution	物流
Distributor	流通業
Dotcom	網路公司
Dress-down day	穿便服日

英文	中文
Duppie (depressed urban professional)	憂鬱的都市專業人員（指過去有高薪或地位的人，現在要從事卑微的工作）
Earnings per share(EPS)	每股稅後純益
Euro	歐元
Ex-all	除權
Ex-dividend	除息
Flexplace	彈性工作場所
Flexecutive	工作時間與地點有彈性的主管或是專業人員
Foreign exchange reserves	外匯存底
Forex designated banks	外匯指定銀行
Ghost brand	過氣的品牌與商標
Pluralist	身兼數職的工作者
Job spill	下班後或是週末假日帶工作回家

● 聽力題中同義字彙的掌握

在聽力的訓練中，了解同義字彙，將可以協助考生快速的選擇出正確的答案，也就是在一般的聽力考試的設計中，我們常發現聽到的內容是「harbor」（港口），但是看到的選項為「port」（港口），或是聽到「customer」（顧客），卻看見「patron」（顧客）的選項，殊不知這些都是同義字，不知這些字便產生了做題目上的障礙，因此多了解聽力字彙中的同義字組，是絕對有其必要性。以下分常見的三十五組同義詞介紹：

◆ 「客人」字彙（**N.**）

英文	中文
Guest	客人，賓客
Client	顧客，客戶
Consumer	消費者；消耗者
Customer	顧客；買主
Patron	主顧（尤指老顧客）

◆ 「忽略」字彙（**V.**）

英文	中文
Overlook	看漏；忽略
Neglect	忽視，忽略
Disregard	忽視
Ignore	忽視
Omit	忽視

◆ 「傑出」字彙（**Adj.**）

英文	中文
Outstanding	顯著的；傑出的；重要的
Eminent	（地位、學識等方面）出眾的，卓越的；著名的
Prominent	卓越的；重要的；著名的
Reputable	聲譽好的，可尊敬的
Noted	有名的
Notable	著名的，顯要的
Renowned	有名的；有聲譽的
Famous	著名的，出名的

英文	中文
Well-known	熟知的
*Notorious	惡名昭彰的，聲名狼藉的

◆ 「展示」字彙（**N.**）

英文	中文
Demonstration	實地示範，實物宣傳
Display	陳列品，展覽品
Fair	商品展覽會；博覽會
Show	展覽，展覽會；陳列品
Exposition	展覽會；博覽會
Exhibit	展示會
Exhibition	展覽；展覽會，展示會

◆ 「比賽」字彙（**N.**）

英文	中文
Race	賽跑；比賽，競賽
Game	競賽；運動會
Match	比賽，競賽
Tourney	比賽；錦標賽
Tournament	比賽；錦標賽；聯賽
Contest	競賽，比賽
Competition	比賽，競賽；賽會

◆ 「手冊」字彙（**N.**）

英文	中文
Brochure	小冊子
Handbook	手冊，便覽
Manual	手冊，便覽，簡介
Directory	姓名住址簿；工商名錄；號碼簿
Pamphlet	小冊子
Booklet	小冊子
Guidebook	旅行指南；手冊

◆ 「設備」字彙（**N.**）

英文	中文
Facility	設備，設施；工具
Device	設備，儀器，裝置
Utensil	器皿，用具
Instrument	儀器；器具，器械
Appliance	器具，用具；裝置，設備
Equipment	設備；器械；用具
Amenities	（常用複數）便利設施，文化設施，福利設施
Comforts	使人舒服的設備，方便的東西
Utility	用品
Apparatus	器械，儀器；設備，裝置

◆ 「商品」字彙（**N.**）

英文	中文
Merchandise	商品，貨物〔U〕

英文	中文
Commodity	商品；日用品
Goods	商品；貨物
Wares	商品，貨物
Product	產品，產物；產量；出產

◆「同伴」字彙（N.）

英文	中文
Company	伴侶（們）；同伴（們），朋友（們）
Companion	同伴，伴侶；朋友
Comrade	夥伴，同事
Mate	同伴，夥伴
Pal	伙伴；好友
Partner	（一起行動的）夥伴，拍檔
Associate	夥伴；同事；朋友；合夥人
Coworker	共同工作者；同事；幫手
Colleague	同事，同僚，同行

◆「公司企業」字彙（N.）

英文	中文
Company	公司，商號
Business	商店；商行；公司；企業
Enterprise	企業，公司
Firm	商號，商行，公司
Industry	工業；企業；行業
Corporation	股份（有限）公司

英文	中文
Conglomerate	企業集團
Empire	大企業
Syndicate	企業聯合組織，財團
Consortium	國際財團；國際借款團
Venture	投機活動；企業

◆ 「合約協議」字彙（**N.**）

英文	中文
Agreement	協定，協議
Accord	（國家之間的）協議；條約
Treaty	約定，協議，契約
Contract	契約
Deal	交易
Pact	契約；協定；條約
Compact	合同，契約
Bargain	協議
Armistice	休戰，停戰休戰（或停戰）協議
Settlement	解決
Lease	租約，租契
Convention	公約，協定

◆ 「收益」字彙（**N.**）

英文	中文
Profit	利潤，盈利；收益，紅利
Yield	產量；收穫量；收益，利潤
Returns	收益，利潤；利息

英文	中文
Proceeds	收益，收入；（期票、保險單等扣除應付費用後的）實收款項
Receipts	收到的物（或款項）；收入
Gains	獲得物；收益，利潤
Income	收入；收益；所得
Revenue	各項收入，總收入
Margin	利潤；賺頭
Earnings	收入，工資
Avail	利潤；（尤指賣掉財產後的）所得

◆ 「企業家」字彙（**N.**）

英文	中文
Enterpriser	企業家；創業者
Entrepreneur	企業家；事業創辦者
Magnate	（實業界的）巨頭，大王；要人，權貴
Tycoon	（企業界的）大亨；巨頭
Industrialist	企業家；工業家；實業家

◆ 「鄉村的」字彙（**Adj.**）

英文	中文
Rural	農村的；田園的；有鄉村風味的
Rustic	鄉村式的；質樸的
Bucolic	鄉下風味的
Countrified	鄉村的；帶鄉村風味的
Provincial	鄉氣的，粗野的；地方性的；偏狹的

◆ 「都市的」字彙（**Adj.**）

英文	中文
Metropolitan	大都市的
Municipal	市的；市政的；市立的，市辦的
Urban	城市的；居住在城市的
Citified	都市風尚的
Civic	城市的

◆ 「服裝」字彙（**N.**）

英文	中文
Clothes	衣服；服裝
Attire	服裝，衣著；盛裝
Apparel	衣服，服裝；衣著
Clothing	（總稱）衣服，衣著
Costume	服裝，裝束
Dress	衣服；（特定的）服裝（如民族服裝，禮服等）
Garment	服裝，衣著
Outfit	（尤指在特殊場合穿的）全套服裝
Wardrobe	（個人的）全部服裝；（劇團的）全部戲裝

◆ 「非專業人士」字彙（**N.**）

英文	中文
Amateur	外行；粗通（某一行）的人
Greener	無經驗的；容易上當的
Rookie	新兵；生手；新入選選手
Apprentice	學徒，徒弟

英文	中文
Novice	新手，初學者
Tyro	初學者；生手；新手
Beginner	初學者，新手；生手
Starter	初學者
Freshman	新人；新手；生手

◆ 「懶惰的」字彙（**Adj.**）

英文	中文
Lazy	懶散的，怠惰的
Inactive	怠惰的；行動緩慢的
Indolent	懶惰的；好逸惡勞的；懶散的
Sluggish	不大想動的；懶散的

◆ 「會議」字彙（**N.**）

英文	中文
Convention	會議，大會；全體與會者
Conference	（正式）會議；討論會，協商會
Meeting	會議；集會；會
Panel discussion	小組的座談會
Hearing	意見聽取會
Congress	（正式）會議；代表大會
Council	會議；政務會；協調會
Seminar	（研究班的）專題討論會
Symposium	討論會；座談會
Forum	公開討論的場所；討論會

英文	中文
Session	會議，集會
Summit	最高官階；最高級會議
Assembly	（大寫）立法機構；議會；（美國有些州的）州議會眾議院
Assemblage	集合在一起的人（或物），集會
Congregation	（宗教的）集會；（教堂的）會眾
Gathering	集會，聚集

◆ 「財產」字彙（**N.**）

英文	中文
Property	財產，資產；所有物
Land	地產，田產
Estate	財產，資產；遺產
Premises	住宅（或辦公室）連全部建築及地基；生產場所，經營場址
Assets	資產，公司所擁有或是應自他人收回，可客觀衡量的權益（如土地、廠房、設備、專利、商譽等。在資產負債表中，通常分為流動資產及非流動資產。）
Capital	資本；本錢
Wealth	財富；財產；資源；富有
Fortune	財產，財富；鉅款

◆ 「特徵」字彙（**N.**）

英文	中文
Characteristic	特性，特徵，特色
Attribute	屬性；特性，特質

英文	中文
Peculiarity	特性，特質
Idiosyncrasy	（個人的）氣質，習性
Trait	特徵，特點，特性
Earmark	特徵
Feature	特徵，特色

◆ 「居民」字彙（N.）

英文	中文
Resident	居民，定居者；僑民
Occupant	占有人；居住者
Dweller	居民；居住者
Inhabitant	（某地區的）居民，居住者
Citizen	市民，（城市）居民，公民
Liver	過著…生活的人，居住者，居民

◆ 「工作」字彙（N.）

英文	中文
Job	工作；職業
Work	工作；勞動；作業；職業，業務
Profession	（尤指受過良好教育或專門訓練者，如律師、醫生、教師的）職業
Occupation	工作，職業
Undertaking	事業；企業；工作

◆ 「協會團體」字彙（**N.**）

英文	中文
Association	協會，公會，社團〔C〕
Organization	組織，機構，團體〔C〕
Society	社團，協會，公會，俱樂部〔C〕
Club	（運動，娛樂等的）俱樂部
Alliance	結盟；聯盟，同盟；聯姻
Cartel	卡特爾，企業聯合
Confederation	同盟，聯盟；邦聯
Federation	聯盟；聯合會

◆ 「稅收」字彙（**N.**）

英文	中文
Tariff	關稅；稅率；關稅表
Tax	稅；稅金
Levy	徵稅，課稅；徵兵
Duty	稅
Impost	稅；關稅

◆ 「拒絕」字彙（**V.**）

英文	中文
Reject	拒絕，抵制
Refuse	拒絕；拒受；拒給；不准
Decline	婉拒；謝絕
Rebuff	斷然拒絕，回絕；冷落
Nix	【俚】不同意；拒絕
Turn down	拒絕（請求等）

◆ 「危險」字彙（**Adj.**）

英文	中文
Dangerous	危險的；不安全的；招致危險的
Hazardous	有危險的；冒險的
Jeopardous	危險的；冒險的
Perilous	危險的；冒險的
Adventurous	愛冒險的；大膽的，充滿危險的；有危險的
Risky	危險的；冒險的；大膽的

◆ 「勤勉」字彙（**Adj.**）

英文	中文
Industrious	勤勉的，勤奮的，勤勞的
Diligent	勤勉的，勤奮的
Sedulous	勤勉的
Hardworking	認真的
Workaholic	醉心於工作的，勤勉的

◆ 「混合」字彙（**V.**）

英文	中文
Blend	使混和，使混雜；使交融
Mix	使混和，摻和
Mingle	使混合，使相混
Merge	使（公司等）合併
Combine	使結合；使聯合
Consolidate	合併，聯合
Unite	聯合；混合

◆ 「區域」字彙（N.）

英文	中文
Region	地區，地帶；行政區域
Zone	地帶；地區
Area	場地，區
District	地區，區域，地帶
Section	地區，區域，地段
Neighborhood	鄰近地區
Territory	領土，版圖；領地
Locality	地區；場所，現場

◆ 「心情差」字彙（Adj.）

英文	中文
Dismal	憂鬱的；沉悶的；淒涼的
Dreary	沉悶的，陰鬱的，令人沮喪的
Dejected	沮喪的，情緒低落的，氣餒的
Miserable	悽慘的；悲哀的
Downhearted	灰心喪氣的，沮喪的
Disheartened	悶悶不樂的，消沉的
Upset	使心煩意亂
Depressed	沮喪的，消沉的，憂鬱的
Gloomy	陰鬱的；憂鬱的
Bleak	淒涼的，陰暗的，無希望的
Joyless	不高興的；沉悶無趣的
Cheerless	不快樂的；陰鬱的；淒涼的

◆ 「證實」字彙（**V.**）

英文	中文
Affirm	證實，確認
Confirm	證實；確定
Prove	證明，證實
Certify	證明，證實
Testify	作證
Verify	證明，證實
Substantiate	證實，證明…有根據

◆ 「活動」字彙（**N.**）

英文	中文
Drive	運動；宣傳活動
Event	事件，大事
Campaign	運動，活動
Movement	（政治、社會、思想）運動

◆ 「指派」字彙（**V.**）

英文	中文
Appoint	任命，指派
Assign	派定，指定，選派
Designate	委任，指派
Name	任命

◆ 「任務」字彙（N.）

英文	中文
Assignment	（分派的）任務；工作
Task	任務；工作；作業
Mission	使命，任務
Duty	責任；義務；本分
Errand	任務，使命

● 聽力相似音，同音異字或同字異音，多重含意字詞掌握

完整的聽力訓練應包括相似音（similar-sounding words），同音異字（Homophone）或同字異音（Heteronym），多重含意（multi-meaning words），同音／同形結尾（Same Suffix）的字詞等。所以我們最後一節的聽力實力養成練習將替讀者分析這些聽力的困擾字。

◆ 相似音（similar-sounding words）

(1)

Ask 問	Axe 斧頭
Bother 麻煩	Brother 兄弟
Card 卡片	Cart 推車
Cloudy 陰天的	Crowded 擁擠的
Die 死亡	Diet 飲食
Found 發現	Fund 基金
Gain 獲得	Game 比賽
Luck 幸運	Lock 鎖
Metal 金屬	Medal 獎章
Menu 菜單	Manual 手冊

Please 請	Police 警察
Pleasure 喜悅	Pressure 壓力
President 總統	Precedent 慣例
Point 要點	Appoint 指派
Restroom 廁所	Restaurant 餐廳
Sigh 嘆息	Sign 簽名

(2)

Apartment 公寓	Department 部門	Appointment 約會
Bush 矮木叢	Brush 刷子	Rush 匆促
Bitter 苦的	Butter 奶油	Better 更好
Contrary 相反	Country 國家	County 縣
Class 班級	Classic 經典	Classical 古典
Consult 諮詢	Console 安慰	Counsel 建議
Dress 洋裝	Address 地址	Dressing 沙拉醬
Father 父親	Further 更進一步的	Farther 更遠的
Flight 班機	Fright 驚恐	Fight 打架
Fall 掉落	Four 四	For 為了
Glass 玻璃	Grace 優雅	Grass 草皮
Dock 碼頭	Deck 甲板	Duck 鴨子
Man 男人	Main 主要的	Men 男性（複數）
Pan 鍋子	Pen 筆	Pain 痛
Order 訂單	Older 較老的	Odor 氣味
Plane 飛機	Plain 樸素的	Plan 計畫
Sour 酸的	Soar 高升	Sore 腫痛
Rice 米	Lice 跳蚤	Nice 好的
Raise 舉起	Praise 讚美	Race 種族

(3)

Expect 預期	Accept 接受	Respect 尊敬	Suspect 懷疑
Hear 聽到	Here 這裡	Heel 腳跟	Hill 山丘
Oppose 反對	Propose 提案	Dispose 拋棄	Suppose 認為
Paw 腳掌	Pole 杆子	Pool 水池	Pull 拉
Wall 牆壁	War 戰爭	World 世界	Word 文字

(1) 相似的母音練習

練習一：請自我唸出以下的單字

1. lock（鎖）/ luck（運氣）
2. fond（喜愛）/ fund（基金）
3. calm（冷靜）/ come（來）
4. pull（拉）/ pool（泳池）
5. foot（足）/ food（食物）
6. stood（站）/ stewed（燉的）
7. back（回去）/ bake（烘烤）
8. ran（跑）/ rain（雨）
9. hat（帽）/ hate（恨）
10. seat（座位）/ sit（坐）
11. deep（深的）/ dip（沾浸）
12. each（每一）/ itch（癢）
13. debt（債）/ date（日期）
14. wet（溼）/ wait（等）
15. test（測驗）/ taste（品嚐）
16. come（來）/ count（計算）
17. ton（噸）/ town（城鎮）
18. nun（修女）/ now（現在）
19. pin（別針）/ pen（筆）
20. will（將）/ well（很好）
21. listen（聽）/ lesson（課程）
22. pen（筆）/ pan（平底鍋）
23. bend（彎曲）/ band（樂團）
24. bed（床）/ bad（壞）
25. ball（球）/ bowl（碗）
26. law（法律）/ low（低）
27. caught（捉）/ coat（外套）
28. bow（弓）/ bow（鞠躬）
29. know（知道）/ now（現在）
30. oat（燕麥）/ out（出去）

練習二：請自我唸出以下的單字

1. chess（棋）/ chase（追逐）/ chance（機會）/ cheese（乳酪）
2. pen（筆）/ pan（平底鍋）/ pain（疼痛）
3. feel（感覺）/ fill（填裝）/ fell（倒下）/ fail（失敗）/ fall（落下）

4. full（充滿）/ fool（傻瓜）

5. beat（擊敗）/ bit（少許）/ bet（打賭）/ bait（餌）/ bat（球棒）

6. ball（球）/ boat（船）

7. lock（鎖）/ luck（運氣）

8. sale（販賣）/ sad（傷心）

9. live（生活）/ leave（離開）

10. ball（球）/ bowl（碗）

(2)相似的子音練習

練習三：請自我唸出以下的單字

1. date（日期）/ late（晚）

2. did（做）/ lid（蓋子）

3. die（死）/ lie（說謊）

4. name（名字）/ main（主要的）

5. gain（得到）/ game（比賽）

6. sun（太陽）/ some（一些）

7. fly（飛）/ fry（煎炒）

8. collect（收集）/ correct（修正）

9. tile（磁磚）/ tire（疲憊）

10. kin（親戚）/ king（國王）

11. ban（限制）/ bang（砰砰聲）

12. thin（瘦）/ thing（事物）

13. ear（耳朵）/ year（年歲）

14. east（東方）/ yeast（酵母）

15. vent（通風）/ went（去）

16. vest（背心）/ west（西方）

17. vine（葡萄藤）/ wine（葡萄酒）

18. need（需要）/ lead（領導）

19. night（夜晚）/ light（輕的）

20. knife（刀子）/ life（生命）

21. sheep（綿羊）/ cheap（便宜）

22. wash（洗）/ watch（觀看）

23. save（拯救）/ shave（刮鬍子）

24. same（相同）/ shame（羞恥）

25. sell（賣）/ shell（外殼）

26. day（天）/ they（他們）

27. dare（膽敢）/ their（他們的）

28. dough（麵糰）/ though（雖然）

29. sing（唱歌）/ thing（事物）

30. face（臉面）/ faith（信心）

31. worse（更糟）/ worth（值得）

32. yell（呼喊）/ jell（凍結）

33. yam（甘藷）/ jam（果醬）

34. yet（尚未）/ jet（噴射機）

35. cheap（便宜）/ jeep（吉普車）

36. choke（窒息）/ joke（笑話）

37. chew（嚼）/ Jew（猶太人）

38. try（嘗試）/ dry（乾燥）

39. train（訓練）/ drain（洩出）

40. trick（惡作劇）/ drink（飲料）

練習四：請自我唸出以下的單字

1. game（遊戲）/ name（名字）　2. slow（緩慢）/ snow（下雪）
3. cold（感冒）/ gold（黃金）　4. rain（下雨）/ train（火車）
5. sun（太陽）/ some（一些）　6. Kim（金）/ king（國王）
7. day（白天）/ date（日期）　8. ready（準備好）/ already（已經）
9. mark（記號）/ market（市場）　10. watch（觀看）/ wash（洗淨）

◆ 同音異字（**Homophone**）

Their 他們的	There 那裡
Know 知道	No 不
Knew 知道（過去式）	New 新的
I 我	Eye 眼睛
Write 寫	Right 正確
Sun 太陽	Son 兒子
Sail 航行	Sale 販售
Sea 海	See 看見
Way 方向	Weigh 秤重
Wait 等待	Weight 重量
Hour 小時	Our 我們的
Male 男性	Mail 郵件
Allowed 允許	Aloud 大聲的
Guest 客人	Guessed 猜測
Higher 更高	Hire 雇用
Pear 梨子	Pair 一對
Cents 分	Sense 感覺
Find 發現	Fined 罰款
Fair 公平的	Fare 車資

Band 樂團	Banned 禁止的
Board 板子	Bored 無聊的
Ad 廣告	Add 增加
Sight 視野	Site 地點
Meat 肉	Meet 遇見
Too 也	Two 二

◆ 同字異音（Heteronym）

❶ contract
- ▶ The sound of the word is con'tracted. 省略（v.）
- ▶ We have to sign this 'contract. 合約（n.）

❷ live
- ▶ I live [ɪ] in the suburb. 住（v.）
- ▶ The live [aɪ] whale is interesting. 活的（adj.）

❸ record
- ▶ He holds the 'record in the high jump. 紀錄（n.）
- ▶ They want to re'cord Charles's class. 錄音（v.）

❹ export
- ▶ He is in the 'export business. 出口（n.）
- ▶ The oranges are ex'ported. 出口（v.）

❺ desert
- ▶ The land without water is a 'desert. 沙漠（n.）
- ▶ The are is de'serted. 遺棄（v.）

⑥ present

▶ He pre′sented the meeting in the end. 出席（v.）

▶ I get a birthday ′present every year. 禮物（n.）

⑦ progress

▶ They pro′gress in their studies. 進展（v.）

▶ They made ′progress. 進展（n.）

⑧ tear

▶ She was moved to tears. [ɪ] 眼淚（n.）

▶ They try to tear [ɛ] down the building. 拆除（v.）

⑨ contest

▶ A speech ′contest will take place soon. 比賽（n.）

▶ He wants to con′test me. 比賽（v.）

⑩ object

▶ We ob′jected to this plan. 反對（v.）

▶ The ′object is really an eyesore. 物體（n.）

◆ 多重含意字（**Multi-meaning words**）

❶ appear

▶ As soon as the shower passed, a rainbow appeared in the sky. 出現（v.）

▶ He appears to be unhappy. 似乎（v.）

❷ book

▶ Put those books on the shelf. 書（n.）

▶ Our hotel is fully booked. 預訂（v.）

❸ **bright**

▶ Always look at the <u>bright</u> side. 明亮的（adj.）

▶ She is a <u>bright</u> girl. 聰明的 （adj.）

❹ **change**

▶ I need to <u>change</u> my diet. 改變（v.）

▶ Here is your <u>change</u>, $2.07. 零錢（n.）

❺ **class**

▶ The <u>class</u> are reading aloud. 學生（n.）

▶ I always take a yoga <u>class</u> after work. 課程（n.）

❻ **company**

▶ ACME is a foreign <u>company</u>. 公司（n.）

▶ She is always my <u>company</u> when I need her. 同伴（n.）

❼ **check**

▶ All passengers need to <u>check</u> their luggage. 檢查（v.）

▶ I'd like to pay my tuition by <u>check</u>. 支票（n.）

❽ **date**

▶ What is the <u>date</u> today? 日期（n.）

▶ She is my <u>date</u>. 約會（的對象）（n.）

❾ **fix**

▶ A repairman is <u>fixing</u> the light. 修理（v.）

▶ My mother has already <u>fixed</u> the dinner. 準備（v.）

❿ **fair**

▶ The trade <u>fair</u> is well-attended. 展覽會（n.）

▶ It is <u>fair</u> today. There is not a cloud in the sky. 晴朗的（adj.）

⑪ **left**

▶ At last, we <u>left</u> without saying goodbye. 離開（v.）

▶ If you turn to the <u>left</u>, you will find our house. 左邊（n.）

⑫ **lie**

▶ Don't tell a <u>lie</u>. 說謊（n.）

▶ <u>Lie</u> on the back. 平躺（v.）

⑬ **light**

▶ The tennis racket is <u>light</u>. 輕的（adj.）

▶ Turn on the <u>light</u>. It's dark inside. 燈（n.）

⑭ **match**

▶ Never play with a <u>match</u>. 火柴（n.）

▶ The tennis <u>match</u> took place yesterday. 比賽（n.）

⑮ **mean**

▶ I didn't <u>mean</u> it. 意思（v.）

▶ The dog is so <u>mean</u>. 凶惡的（adj.）

⑯ **note**

▶ I lost my <u>notes</u> from the meeting. 會議紀錄（n.）

▶ This is a ten-pond <u>note</u>. 紙鈔（n.）

⑰ **train**

▶ The swimmers are in <u>training</u>. 訓練（n.）

▶ The <u>train</u> is coming up quickly. 火車（n.）

⑱ **plant**

▶ The gardener is <u>planting</u> flowers in the garden. 種植（v.）

▶ The company has some <u>plants</u> overseas. 工廠（n.）

⑲ **rest**

▶ I am exhausted. I need some <u>rest</u>. 休息（n.）

▶ Are you sure he is the man that you want to live for the <u>rest</u> of your life? 剩餘（n.）

⑳ **address**

▶ Give his your <u>address</u>. 地址（n.）

▶ She is <u>addressing</u> the group. 演說（v.）

㉑ **meet**

▶ We <u>meet</u> every weekend. 遇見（v.）

▶ They are running in the <u>meet</u>. 運動會（n.）

㉒ **minute**

▶ Wait a <u>minute</u>. 分鐘（n.）

▶ I need the board <u>minutes</u>. 會議紀錄（n.）

㉓ **fine**

My parents are <u>fine</u>. 很好的（adj.）

The <u>fine</u> will be imposed soon. 罰款（n.）

㉔ **kind**

It's very <u>kind</u> of you to say that. 仁慈的（adj.）

What <u>kind</u> of movies do you like? 種類（n.）

㉕ **plain**

I want to order a <u>plain</u> pizza. 普通的（adj.）

Beyond the <u>plain</u> is a high hill. 平原（n.）

🔊 **fall**

Do not <u>fall</u> off the bike. 掉落（v.）

I like the weather in <u>fall</u>. 秋天（n.）

◆ 同形結尾（Same Suffix）

(1) 第一組 -sion

Session 期別	Mission 大使	Passion 熱情	Vision 視力
Possession 所有物	Dimension 方面	Profession 職業	Division 部門
Supervision 監督	Intermission 暫停	Comprehension 理解	Revision 修正

(2) 第二組 -tion

Auction 拍賣	Nation 國家	Fiction 虛構	Caution 小心
Production 生產	Perfection 完美	Instruction 指導	Pollution 污染
Regulation 規則	Education 教育	Preparation 準備	Compensation 補償

(3) 第三組 -ent

Accent 口音	Urgent 緊急	Current 目前	Moment 時刻
Evident 明顯的	Precedent 先例	Confident 自信的	Apparent 明顯的
Entertainment 娛樂	Convenient 方便的	Encouragement 鼓勵	Experiment 實驗

(4) 第四組 -ive

Alive 活著的	Native 出生地的	Survive 生存	Active 活躍的
Progressive 漸進的	Impressive 印象深刻的	Attentive 注意的	Sensitive 敏感的
Comparative 比較的	Preservative 保存的	Conservative 保守的	Imperative 必要的

(5) 第五組 -al

National 國家的	Loyal 忠誠的	Social 社會的	Journal 期刊
Industrial 工業的	Digital 數字的	Natural 自然的	Festival 節慶
Economical 節約的	Professional 專業的	Mechanical 機器的	Fundamental 基礎的

(6) 第六組 -ate

Create 創造	Translate 翻譯	Climate 氣候	Relate 敘述
Terminate 終結	Fascinate 迷幻	Decorate 裝飾	Affectionate 親切的
Appreciate 感激	Eliminate 排除	Cooperate 合作	Investigate 調查

(7) 第七組 -ic

Public 公共的	Magic 魔術	Panic 恐慌	Plastic 塑膠的
Cosmestic 化妝的	Pacific 和平的	Terrific 很棒的	Electric 電力的
Enthusiastic 熱忱的	Automatic 自動的	Academic 學術的	Energetic 有活力的

(8) 第八組-ous

Jealous 忌妒的	Famous 有名的	Nervous 緊張的	Precious 寶貴的
Dangerous 危險的	Generous 慷慨的	Various 多樣的	Delicious 美味的
Ridiculous 可笑的	Harmonious 和諧的	Mysterious 神祕的	Ambiguous 含糊不清的

(9) 第九組-ise

Concise 精簡的	Precise 準確的	Despise 輕視	Advise 忠告
Advertise 廣告	Compromise 妥協	Exercise 運動	Revise 修正

(10) 第十組-ry

Angry 生氣的	Hungry 餓的	Hurry 緊急的	Hairy 多毛的
Factory 工廠	Chemistry 化學	Industry 工業	Primary 最初的
Secretary 祕書	Necessary 必要的	January 一月	February 二月

筆記頁

聽力題目實戰練習 (PART 2)

聽力考試時要注意的事項

　　首先，要利用題目作答說明播放的時間。因為我們在平時的模擬試題練習中，早就對各個大題的作答說明十分熟悉，因此在作答說明時，就是瀏覽題目或圖片的最佳時機，並且最好能預測圖片或是對話的背景，延伸你的想像力。圖片題時要注意人物的動作，職業身分與相互關係。物件題則注意東西的形體與相互對比的位置。問答題時，要注意相似音字（similar-sounding words）的混淆。問句出現過的字，若在答句又出現一次或是出現相似音的字，通常是「不正確」的答案。對話題與短文題要先瀏覽題目再聽內容，至少要把相關疑問詞先看一遍，知道是問時間，地點或是身分。答案的選擇盡量採用刪去法，也就是先剔除錯的答案，再進行選擇。真的不確定答案也要猜一個選項，再定下心來準備下一題。

看圖辨義

為了測試應試者能對於所見的事物，作正確清楚的表達，一般考試的聽力測驗都會有看圖或看照片的測驗題型。其中多益（TOEIC）考試以真實的照片（Photograph）來出題，而英檢（GEPT）或是大學入學英語聽力測驗則是以手繪圖片（picture）來出題。兩者的概念大同小異，目的都是要考出考生對於所見的事物有正確描述（description）的能力。

■ 本章重點
- 看圖聽選項（一圖一題）
- 看圖聽選項（一圖多題）

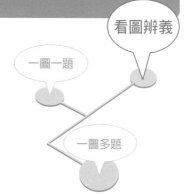

● 看圖聽選項（一圖一題）

英文看圖辨義的第一種方式，就是一圖配一題。在這種題型中，考生要仔細看清楚圖片（或照片）裡的人事物。在人物題的部分，要注意人的動作以及他（她）的相關穿著；在物件題的部分，則要特別注意物品的相對位置關係。出題方式：題本上只看到圖片，題目與選項則由CD播出，不印製在試題本上。此類題型多為多益（TOEIC）的出題方式。以下1～20題以照片（photo）的方式呈現，此為多益考題方式；21～35題以圖片（picture）的方式呈現，此為英檢考試的方式。

◆ 聽力測驗試題1～35題（請聽CD播放選項，並將答案寫在圖片旁 ⊙ 4-01）

1.

2.

3.

4.

5.

6.

7.

8.

9.

10.

11.

12.

13.

14.

15.

16.

17.

18.

19.

20.

21.

22.

23.

24.

25.

26.

27.

28.

29.

30.

31.

32.

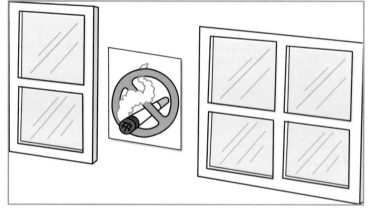

33.

34.

35.

*看圖聽選項（一圖一題）1-35題解答請見 141 頁。

● 看圖聽選項（一圖多題）

英文看圖辨義的第二種方式，就是一圖配多題。在這種題型中，考生要仔細看清楚圖片（或照片）裡的人、事、物。由於是一圖配多題，所以圖中的每一個細節都要注意，例如人物的角色，相對位置與服飾；人物附近的物品也需仔細的觀察。出題方式：題本上只看到圖片，題目與選項則由CD播出，不印製在試題本上。此類題型多為英檢的出題方式。

◆ 聽力測驗試題36～60題（請聽CD播放選項，並將答案寫在圖片旁 ⊙ 4-02）

Picture A.（36～38題）

連續圖

Kelly Wang

Picture B.（39～41題）

地圖一張Tina的家。

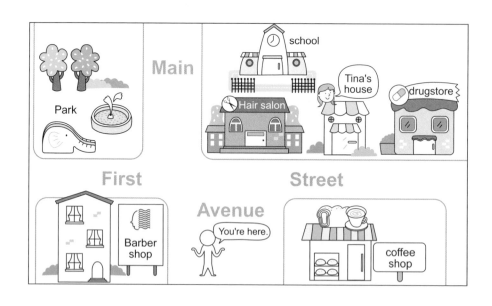

Picture C.（42～44題）

Picture D.（45～46題）

Picture E.（47～49題）

Picture F.（50～51題）

Picture G.（52～53題）

Picture H.（54～55題）

Picture I.（56〜57題）

Picture U.（58〜60題）

*看圖聽選項（一圖多題）36-60題解答請見第 155 頁。

■解答

◆看圖聽選項（一圖一題）聽力測驗試題敘述內容與解答1～35題

（A）1.

    A. The man is sitting in front of the computer.

    B. The man is enjoying his lunch in the office.

    C. The man is talking to a client on the phone.

    D. The man is rehearsing a play on the stage.

（C）2.

    A. The woman is looking for her mobile phone.

    B. The woman is hanging up the phone.

    C. The woman is speaking into the microphone.

    D. The woman is looking at the man.

（C）3.

    A. The man is drowning in the sea.

    B. The man is trying to catch some fish.

    C. The man is reading something in his hands.

    D. The man is standing by the sea.

（D）4.

    A. The booth is on the corner.

    B. The sign is being torn down.

    C. The driver is sighing.

    D. There are some words on the sign.

（C）5.

    A. There's much traffic on the road.

    B. A man is riding a bike.

    C. There is a street sign.

    D. Some joggers are running along the road.

（B）6.

　　　A. The man at the podium is watching a film.

　　　B. The man is addressing the group.

　　　C. The man is leaning against the wall.

　　　D. The man is filling out the application form.

（C）7.

　　　A. The plane is at its gate.

　　　B. The crane is on the marina.

　　　C. The train is at the station.

　　　D. The yacht is on the sea.

（D）8.

　　　A. They are holding the helmets.

　　　B. They are getting their motorcycle serviced.

　　　C. They are measuring the height of the sculpture.

　　　D. They are riding motorbikes.

（A）9.

　　　A. Some shoes are on display.

　　　B. The bookshelf is empty.

　　　C. The globe is in the bookcase.

　　　D. The plant is near the wall.

（A）10.

　　　A. They are all sitting on the chairs.

　　　B. They are standing in front of the computer.

　　　C. The table is being cleaned.

　　　D. Only three people are sitting around the table.

（C）11.

    A. They are shaking hands.

    B. They are sitting down.

    C. They are waiting in line to board the ferry.

    D. They are eating dinner.

（C）12.

    A. The office is all vacant.

    B. The desks are in a circle.

    C. The desk is set with computers.

    D. The wastebaskets are next to the desk.

（D）13.

    A. Two men are talking.

    B. All seats are occupied.

    C. They are sitting on the sofa.

    D. There is a pillow on the sofa.

（C）14.

    A. It's raining heavily.

    B. A car is driving along on the street.

    C. Snow covers the car.

    D. People are having a snowball fight.

（C）15.

    A. They are waiting for the traffic light.

    B. They are dancing.

    C. They are facing each other.

    D. They are holding a cup of coffee.

（D）16.

　　　　A. They are buying some ink cartridges.

　　　　B. They are buying some fruit in the market.

　　　　C. They are pouring some fresh juice.

　　　　D. They are filling out something.

（C）17.

　　　　A. They are holding the bag together.

　　　　B. They are buying some backpacks.

　　　　C. They are walking down the stairs.

　　　　D. They are weighing something on the scale.

（A）18.

　　　　A. Some ducks are on the grass.

　　　　B. Some trees are fallen down.

　　　　C. Heavy snow covers the highway.

　　　　D. People are walking in the rain.

（D）19.

　　　　A. The bed needs to be made.

　　　　B. The housekeeper is making the bed.

　　　　C. The hotel room is occupied.

　　　　D. The hotel room is ready for occupancy.

（A）20.

　　　　A. Cars are driving along the road.

　　　　B. Planes are taking off.

　　　　C. Passengers are getting on the bus.

　　　　D. Boats are crossing the stream.

（A）21.

    A. The swimmer is swimming in the pool.

    B. The gardener is watering some plants.

    C. The shopper is buying a bottle of water.

    D. The guest is relaxing by the pool.

（C）22.

    A. The farmer is growing vegetables.

    B. The office worker is preparing his meal.

    C. The chef is cooking in the kitchen.

    D. The manager is filing the documents.

（B）23.

    A. She is taking a photograph.

    B. She is photocopying some documents.

    C. She is sending a copy of the report.

    D. She is fixing the copy machine.

（B）24.

    A. The man is parking his car in the garage.

    B. The man is riding a motorcycle along the road.

    C. The man is bicycling in the field.

    D. Both men are riding a bike.

（C）25.

    A. The woman is sitting at the desk.

    B. The woman is signing a birthday card.

    C. The woman is wiping the table.

    D. The woman is vacuuming the rug.

（C）26.

    A. The tourist is checking in at the counter.

    B. The inspector is doing a thorough check.

    C. The patron is paying the check.

    D. The author is checking some mistakes.

（A）27.

    A. The man is reading at his desk.

    B. The man is buying a brochure.

    C. The man is arranging some books.

    D. The man is storing food in jars.

（C）28.

    A. The woman is cleaning out the wastebasket.

    B. The woman is picking up some trash.

    C. The woman is pointing at the garbage can.

    D. The woman is littering in the office.

（D）29.

    A. The office worker is working at the desk.

    B. The architect is discussing the floor plan.

    C. The plumber is fixing the leaking sink.

    D. The mail carrier is delivering a package.

（D）30.

    A. The assistant is collecting the toll.

    B. The barking dog is running after the thief.

    C. The driver is paying for the parking fee.

    D. The motorist is stopping by the traffic light.

（A）31.

    A. The woman is serving the customers.

    B. The woman is washing the plates.

    C. The woman is holding a pen.

    D. The woman is cooking.

（A）32.

    A. The sign is between the windows.

    B. The sign is fallen over.

    C. The windows are broken.

    D. The barrel is above the sign.

（D）33.

    A. She is working on the computer.

    B. The computer is turned off.

    C. Some workers are helping each other.

    D. She is watching television.

（A）34.

    A. He is polishing the vehicle.

    B. He is sitting by the vehicle.

    C. He is driving a car.

    D. He is hailing a taxi.

（A）35.

    A. The woman is paying the cashier.

    B. The woman is writing a check.

    C. The cashier is standing in front of a display case.

    D. The cashier is brewing some coffee.

◆ 看圖聽選項（一圖一題）聽力測驗試題中文翻譯1～35題

1.

　　A. 男士正坐在電腦前。

　　B. 男士正在辦公室享受他的午餐。

　　C. 男士正在跟顧客講電話。

　　D. 男士正在舞臺上預演一齣劇。

2.

　　A. 女士正在找她的手機。

　　B. 女士正在掛電話。

　　C. 女士正對著麥克風說話。

　　D. 女士正在看這位男士。

3.

　　A. 男士快要在海中溺斃。

　　B. 男士正試著抓魚。

　　C. 男士正在讀他手上的東西。

　　D. 男士正站在海邊。

4.

　　A. 電話亭在角落。

　　B. 招牌正在被拆除。

　　C. 駕駛員正在嘆氣。

　　D. 標示上有一些文字。

5.

　　A. 路上交通繁忙。

　　B. 男士正在騎單車。

　　C. 有路牌。

　　D. 一些慢跑者沿路跑步。

6.

    A. 講臺上的男士正在看影片。

    B. 男士正在對一群人說話。

    C. 男士正在靠牆。

    D. 男士正在填寫表格。

7.

    A. 飛機在登機門前。

    B. 起重機在碼頭。

    C. 火車在車站。

    D. 帆船在海上。

8.

    A. 他們正握著安全帽。

    B. 他們正讓別人修理他們的機車。

    C. 他們正在測量雕像的高度。

    D. 他們正在騎著機車。

9.

    A. 一些鞋子在展示。

    B. 書架是空的。

    C. 地球儀在書櫃裡。

    D. 植物盆栽在牆壁旁。

10.

    A. 他們全都坐在椅子上。

    B. 他們站在電腦前。

    C. 桌子清潔過了。

    D. 只有三個人坐在桌子旁。

11.

    A. 他們正在握手。

    B. 他們都坐在椅子上。

    C. 他們正在排隊登渡輪。

    D. 他們正在吃晚餐。

12.

    A. 辦公室是空的。

    B. 桌子呈現圓型排列。

    C. 桌子設置電腦。

    D. 垃圾桶在辦公桌旁。

13.

    A. 兩位男士在交談。

    B. 所有座位均有人坐著。

    C. 他們坐在沙發上。

    D. 沙發上有一個靠墊。

14.

    A. 雨下得很大。

    B. 一輛車在街上跑。

    C. 雪覆蓋著車子。

    D. 人們在打雪仗。

15.

    A. 他們正在等紅綠燈。

    B. 他們正在跳舞。

    C. 他們面對著彼此。

    D. 他們手上握著一杯咖啡。

16.
  A. 他們正在買一些墨水匣。
  B. 他們正在市場買一些水果。
  C. 他們正在倒一些新鮮的果汁。
  D. 他們正在填寫東西。

17.
  A. 他們一起提著一個袋子。
  B. 他們正在買背包。
  C. 他們正在下樓。
  D. 他們正在磅秤上秤重。

18.
  A. 一些鴨子在草地上。
  B. 一些樹木倒下。
  C. 大雪覆蓋整個高速公路。
  D. 人們正走在雨中。

19.
  A. 床需要被整裡。
  B. 清潔人員正在整理床鋪。
  C. 旅館房間有人使用。
  D. 旅館房間準備好讓房客住進了。

20.
  A. 車子在馬路上奔馳。
  B. 飛機正在起飛。
  C. 乘客正在上公車。
  D. 船正橫越小溪。

21.

    A. 泳客正在泳池內游泳。

    B. 園丁在替植物澆水。

    C. 購物者正在買一瓶水。

    D. 客人正在泳池旁休息。

22.

    A. 農夫正在種菜。

    B. 辦公室人員正在準備他的餐點。

    C. 廚師正在廚房煮飯。

    D. 經理正在歸檔檔案。

23.

    A. 她正在照相。

    B. 她正在影印文件。

    C. 她正在寄送一份報告。

    D. 她正在修理影印機。

24.

    A. 男士正把車停在車庫。

    B. 男士正沿著馬路騎機車。

    C. 男士正在廣場騎單車。

    D. 兩位男士正在騎單車。

25.

    A. 女士正坐在桌子前。

    B. 女士正在寫一張生日卡。

    C. 女士正在擦桌子。

    D. 女士正在用吸塵器吸地毯。

26.

    A. 觀光客正在櫃檯報到。

    B. 監工正在做仔細的檢查。

    C. 客人正在付帳。

    D. 作者正在檢查錯誤。

27.

    A. 男士正在桌前閱讀。

    B. 男士正在買手冊。

    C. 男士正在整理書。

    D. 男士正把食物存在罐子中。

28.

    A. 女士正在清理垃圾桶。

    B. 女士正在收垃圾。

    C. 女士正指著垃圾桶。

    D. 女士正在辦公室丟垃圾。

29.

    A. 辦公室工作者正在桌子前工作。

    B. 建築師正在討論平面圖。

    C. 水管工正在修理漏水的水槽。

    D. 郵差正在配送包裹。

30.

    A. 助理正在收錢。

    B. 吠叫的狗正在追小偷。

    C. 駕駛正在付停車費。

    D. 駕駛正在紅綠燈前暫停。

31.

　　A. 女士為客人送餐。

　　B. 女士正在洗碗盤。

　　C. 女士拿著一枝筆。

　　D. 女士正在作菜。

32.

　　A. 告示牌在兩個窗戶中間。

　　B. 告示牌掉下來了。

　　C. 窗戶破了。

　　D. 桶子在告示牌的上方。

33.

　　A. 她正在電腦前工作。

　　B. 電腦關機了。

　　C. 工人們正在互相幫助。

　　D. 她正在看電視。

34.

　　A. 他把車打蠟。

　　B. 他坐在汽車旁。

　　C. 他正在開車。

　　D. 他正在招計程車。

35.

　　A. 女人正在付錢結帳。

　　B. 女人正寫支票。

　　C. 收銀員在櫃檯前工作。

　　D. 收銀員正在煮咖啡。

◆ 看圖聽選項（一圖多題）聽力測驗試題敘述內容與解答36～60題

For questions number 36, 37 and 38, please look at picture A.

Question number 36:

（A）Which statement is true about the place?

A. It's a hotel.

B. It's a shopping center.

C. It's a service station.

D. It's a studio.

Question number 37:

（D）Please look at picture A again. What might the receptionist say to Kelly?

A. I have a reservation for tonight and tomorrow night.

B. Ms. Wang, your seat is 210 on the right.

C. Here, you need my key to open the office. I've locked it.

D. Here is your key, ma'am. Your room is on the second floor.

Question number 38:

（A）Please look at picture A again. Which description matches the picture?

A. First, Kelly talked to the clerk at the counter. Then, she took the elevator to the second floor. After that, she opened the door to Room 210 and walked in.

B. First, at 2:30, Kelly talked to the receptionist. Then, she waited for the escalator to go to the second floor. After that, at 3:00, she walked into Room 210.

C. First, Kelly rode on the elevator to the second floor. Then, she opened Room 210. After that, she walked downstairs to ask the clerk some questions.

D. First, Kelly took the stairs to the second floor. Then, she talked to the receptionist by the counter. After that, she took the elevator at 2:50.

For questions number 39 , 40 and 41, please look at picture B.

Question number 39:

（C） Where is the barber shop?

A. It's next to the school.

B. It's around the corner from the hair salon.

C. It's across from the coffee shop.

D. It's between the hair salon and the drugstore.

Question number 40:

（C） What does the map show?

A. The barber shop is across from the drugstore.

B. The park is next to the school.

C. The coffee shop is on the corner of Main Ave and First Street.

D. The hair salon is between the coffee shop and the barber shop.

Question number 41:

（D） Look at the map again. How can I get to Tina's place?

A. Walk up the First Street and turn right on Main Ave.

B. Walk along Main Ave and turn right on First Street. Tina's house is on the right between the hair salon and the drugstore.

C. Walk up the First Street for 2 blocks, and Tina's house is on your left.

D. Walk along Main Ave and turn right on First Street. Tina's house is on the left between the hair salon and the drugstore.

For questions number 42, 43 and 44, please look at picture C.

Question number 42:

（C） Which of the following descriptions is true?

A. The woman is wearing a shirt and pants.

B. The woman is carrying three boxes.

C. The man is wearing trousers.

D. The man is carrying two boxes.

Question number 43:

(C) What is the woman doing?

    A. She's lifting weights and doing her exercises.

    B. She's rock climbing and lifting boxes.

    C. She's climbing the stairs and carrying things.

    D. She's getting in the man's way.

Question number 44: Look at picture C again.

(C) What might the woman say to the man?

    A. Can you get out of my house?

    B. Why don't you give me some ideas?

    C. Can you do me a favor? I can't carry them myself.

    D. Oh, boy. There he goes again.

For question number 45 and 46, please look at picture D.

Question number 45:

(D) Where might John be now?

    A. He is in the Internet café.

    B. He is in the police station.

    C. He is in the dentist's office.

    D. He is in the post office.

Question number 46: Look at Window B.

(A) What might the clerk say to John?

    A. Does it include any valuables, like bracelets or cash?

    B. I want to buy some envelopes and postage stamps.

    C. Can you cash the check for me? I need some cash right away.

    D. Please remember to mail the letter before you leave.

For questions number 47, 48 and 49, please look at picture E.

Question number 47:

(D) How many people are there in the living room?

 A. six.

 B. five.

 C. four.

 D. three.

Question number 48: Look at picture E again.

(D) What do you see on the table?

 A. A coffee cup, a hot pot and a vase.

 B. A coffee pot, a vase and a dog.

 C. A coffee pot, two caps and some flour.

 D. A coffee pot, a vase and two cups.

Question number 49: Look at picture E again.

(B) Which of the following descriptions is "NOT" true about the picture?

 A. There are three people in the living room.

 B. Lucy is walking her dog.

 C. Mr. Lee is busy mopping the floor.

 D. Mrs. Lee is wiping the windows.

For questions number 50 and 51, please look at picture F.

Question number 50:

(C) What description is correct?

 A. Tammy and Gary are eating in the parking lot.

 B. There are two birds under the tree.

 C. Today is a fair day. There is not a cloud in the sky.

 D. The wooden bench by the path is occupied.

Question number 51: Look at picture F again.

（B） What is the place?

　　A. An auditorium.

　　B. A park.

　　C. A parking lot.

　　D. A stadium.

For questions number 52 and 53, please look at picture G.

Question number 52:

（B） What is the place?

　　A. An employee lounge.

　　B. A conference room.

　　C. A ballroom.

　　D. A cafeteria.

Question number 53: Look at picture G again.

（B） What might the man say to the other people sitting around the table?

　　A. Let's welcome Mr. Chi to perform a violin concerto.

　　B. I am happy to announce that the profits this quarter have improved a lot.

　　C. If you examine it carefully, you will find the fine brushwork the painter used.

　　D. Roast beef and grilled fish are our today's specials. Would you like an appetizer to start?

For questions number 54 and 55, please look at picture H.

Question number 54:

（D） What is this place?

　　A. An airport.

　　B. A bus stop.

C. A museum.

D. An MRT train.

Question number 55: Look at picture H again.

（D） What are the people doing in this place?

A. They are getting off the plane.

B. They are walking in the rain.

C. They are waiting in line.

D. They are boarding the train.

For questions number 56 and 57, please look at picture I.

Question number 56:

（D） What is this place?

A. A tennis court.

B. A ballroom.

C. A fitting room.

D. A basketball court.

Question number 57: Look at picture I again.

（B） Which statement is correct?

A. They are practicing jumping.

B. They are having a basketball game.

C. They are watching an exciting ball game.

D. They are releasing a balloon into the sky.

For questions number 58, 59 and 60, please look at picture U.

Question number 58:

（D） What kind of advertisement is it?

A. It's about studying overseas.

B. It's about selling motors.

C. It's about selling computers.

D. It's about a tour.

Question number 59: Look at picture U again.

（D） Who would be interested in this ad?

A. A person who wants to have his computer repaired.

B. A person who wants to learn cooking.

C. A person who wants to make a foreign friend.

D. A person who wants to take an overseas trip.

Question number 60: Look at picture U again.

（A） What statement is "NOT" true?

A. It costs $38000 for a 4-day trip to Japan.

B. It costs $42000 for a 5-day trip to Korea.

C. It costs $38000 for a 6-day trip to China.

D. The trip to Korea is the most expensive.

◆ 看圖聽選項（一圖多題）聽力測驗試題中文翻譯36～60題

問題36，37與問題38請看照片A

36. 下列有關地點的敘述何者爲是？

A. 旅館。

B. 購物中心。

C. 加油站。

D. 錄音室。

37. 服務人員可能會跟凱莉說什麼？

A. 我今晚與明晚有預約。

B. 王小姐，你的座位是右手邊210號。

C. （鑰匙在）這裡，你需要我的鑰匙去打開辦公室的門，我已經鎖門了。

D. 女士，這是你的鑰匙。你的房間在二樓。

38. 下列哪一個敘述符合圖片？

A. 首先，凱莉對櫃檯的服務生說話。然後，她搭電梯到二樓。之後，她打開210室的門並走進去。

B. 首先，在2:30時，凱莉對櫃檯的服務生說話。然後，她等手扶梯到二樓。之後，在3:00，她走進210室。

C. 首先，凱莉搭電梯到二樓。之後，她打開210室的門。之後，走下樓去問服務人員一些問題。

D. 首先，凱莉走樓梯到二樓。然後，凱莉對櫃檯的服務生說話。之後，她在2:50時搭電梯。

問題39，40與問題41請看照片B

39. 男士理髮廳在哪裡？

A. 它在學校旁。

B. 它在沙龍轉角處。

C. 它在咖啡廳對面。

D. 它在美髮沙龍與藥局之間。

40. 地圖展示出什麼訊息？

　　A. 理髮聽在藥局的對面。

　　B. 公園在學校的旁邊。

　　C. 咖啡廳在主要大道與第一街兩路的路口。

　　D. 美髮沙龍在咖啡廳與理髮廳之間。

41. 我要怎麼去蒂娜的家？

　　A. 走到第一街，在主要大道上右轉。

　　B. 沿著主要大道走，第一街時右轉，蒂娜的家在右手邊，
　　　　在美髮沙龍與藥局之間。

　　C. 走兩個街區到第一街，蒂娜的家就在你的左手邊。

　　D. 沿著主要大道走，第一街時右轉，蒂娜的家在左手邊，
　　　　在美髮沙龍與藥局之間。

問題42，43與問題44請看照片C

42. 下列何者敘述正確？

　　A. 女士穿著襯衫與長褲。

　　B. 女士拿三個箱子。

　　C. 男士穿著長褲。

　　D. 男士拿兩個箱子。

43. 女士正在做什麼？

　　A. 她正在舉重與作運動。

　　B. 她正在攀岩與抬箱子。

　　C. 她正在爬樓梯與拿東西。

　　D. 她正擋著男士的去路。

44. 這女子可能對這男子說什麼？

　　A. 你可否離開我的房子？

　　B. 你為何不給我一些想法？

C. 你可否幫忙？我自己無法抬。

D. 天呀，他又來了。

問題45與問題46請看照片D

45. 約翰現在可能在哪？

    A. 網咖。

    B. 警局。

    C. 牙醫診所。

    D. 郵局。

46. 郵局人員可能對約翰說什麼？

    A. 有沒有包含有價物，如手鐲或是現金的？

    B. 我想要買一些信封與郵票。

    C. 可以替我兌現這張支票？我現在需要一些現金。

    D. 離開前請記得寄信。

問題47，48與問題49請看照片E

47. 客廳一共有幾人？

    A. 六人。

    B. 五人。

    C. 四人。

    D. 三人。

48. 你在桌上看到什麼？

    A. 一個咖啡杯，一個熱壺與一個花瓶。

    B. 一個咖啡壺，一個花瓶與一隻狗。

    C. 一個咖啡壺，兩個帽子與一些麵粉。

    D. 一個咖啡壺，一個花瓶與兩個杯子。

49. 哪一項敘述不是真的？

    A. 有三人現在在客廳。

    B. 露西正在遛狗。

    C. 李先生正忙著拖地。

    D. 李太太正在擦窗。

問題50與問題51請看照片F

50. 哪一項敘述為真？

    A. 譚咪與蓋瑞正在停車場吃飯。

    B. 在樹下有兩隻鳥。

    C. 今天是個晴朗日。天空沒有一片雲。

    D. 小路旁的長凳子有人坐。

51. 這是什麼地方？

    A. 禮堂。

    B. 公園。

    C. 停車場。

    D. 體育館。

問題52與問題53請看照片G

52. 這是什麼地方？

    A. 員工休息室。

    B. 會議室。

    C. 宴會廳。

    D. 自助餐廳。

53. 這位男士可能對坐在桌子周圍的人說些什麼？

    A. 讓我們歡迎齊先生表演小提琴協奏曲。

    B. 我很高興的宣布這一季的利潤改善很多。

    C. 假如你仔細檢視，你會看見畫匠的精細畫工。

    D. 烤牛肉與烤魚是今日特餐。你要先來個甜點嗎？

問題54與問題55請看照片H

54. 這是什麼地方？
    A. 機場。
    B. 公車站。
    C. 博物館。
    D. 捷運車內。

55. 人們在這地方做什麼？
    A. 他們正在下飛機。
    B. 他們正走在雨中。
    C. 他們正在排隊。
    D. 他們正在上火車。

問題56與問題57請看照片I

56. 這是什麼地方？
    A. 網球場。
    B. 宴會廳。
    C. 更衣室。
    D. 籃球場。

57. 下列敘述何者為真？
    A. 他們正在練習跳。
    B. 他們正在進行籃球賽。
    C. 他們正在看一場刺激的球賽。
    D. 他們正在放出氣球到空中。

問題58，59與問題60請看照片U

58. 這是什麼樣的廣告？
    A. 有關海外留學。
    B. 有關賣車。

C. 有關賣電腦。

D. 有關旅行。

59. 誰會對這廣告有興趣？

A. 想修電腦的人。

B. 想學烹飪的人。

C. 想交外國友人的人。

D. 想到國外旅遊的人。

60. 哪一項敘述不是真的？

A. 到日本四天行38000元。

B. 到韓國5日42000元。

C. 到中國6日38000元。

D. 到韓國的旅程最貴。

筆記頁

問答題

問答題的設計是在測驗考生對於英語的應對理解力（Listening Comprehension）。這類的考題很普遍，包括多益（TOEIC），英檢（GEPT）以及高中英語聽力學測，通通涵蓋在內。其中多益（TOEIC）的題型是題目與選項都要用聽的，試題本上沒有任何的敘述。而英檢（GEPT）以及高中英語聽力學測，則是聽到問的題目，答的選項則出現在試題本上，要使用閱讀的方式來完成作答。

■ 本章重點

● 問答題一（問與答都聽）

● 問答題二（問句聽，答句讀）

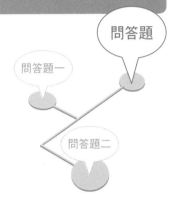

● 問答題一（問與答都聽）

　　問答題一，即一個問題（或直述句）配三個選項，問題與回答的選項均由CD播出，不會出現在試題本上。這種題型，以多益（TOEIC）聽力的考試為主。考題有分疑問句（又分Yes-No問句，疑問詞WH的問句以及選擇性or的問句，或是附加問句（Tag Question））以及直述句。以下請聽CD練習30題模擬試題。

◆ 聽力測驗試題1～30題 5-01（請將答案畫入答案卡內）

答 案 卡

1. 請使用2B鉛筆作答。
2. 畫記要粗黑、清晰，不可超出框線，擦拭要清潔，若畫記過輕或污損不清，不為機器所接受，考生自行負責。
3. 答案須修改時，請用橡皮擦，勿使用立可白或其他修正液。

1	Ⓐ Ⓑ Ⓒ	16	Ⓐ Ⓑ Ⓒ
2	Ⓐ Ⓑ Ⓒ	17	Ⓐ Ⓑ Ⓒ
3	Ⓐ Ⓑ Ⓒ	18	Ⓐ Ⓑ Ⓒ
4	Ⓐ Ⓑ Ⓒ	19	Ⓐ Ⓑ Ⓒ
5	Ⓐ Ⓑ Ⓒ	20	Ⓐ Ⓑ Ⓒ
6	Ⓐ Ⓑ Ⓒ	21	Ⓐ Ⓑ Ⓒ
7	Ⓐ Ⓑ Ⓒ	22	Ⓐ Ⓑ Ⓒ
8	Ⓐ Ⓑ Ⓒ	23	Ⓐ Ⓑ Ⓒ
9	Ⓐ Ⓑ Ⓒ	24	Ⓐ Ⓑ Ⓒ
10	Ⓐ Ⓑ Ⓒ	25	Ⓐ Ⓑ Ⓒ
11	Ⓐ Ⓑ Ⓒ	26	Ⓐ Ⓑ Ⓒ
12	Ⓐ Ⓑ Ⓒ	27	Ⓐ Ⓑ Ⓒ
13	Ⓐ Ⓑ Ⓒ	28	Ⓐ Ⓑ Ⓒ
14	Ⓐ Ⓑ Ⓒ	29	Ⓐ Ⓑ Ⓒ
15	Ⓐ Ⓑ Ⓒ	30	Ⓐ Ⓑ Ⓒ

*問答題一解答請見第 178 頁。

● 問答題二（問句聽，答句讀）

　　問答題二，即一個問題（或直述句）配四個選項，問題由CD播出，選項則在試題本上。這種題型，以全民英檢GEPT以及高中學測聽力的考試為主。考題一樣有分疑問句（又分Yes-No問句，疑問詞WH的問句以及選擇性or的問句，或是附加問句（Tag Question））以及直述句。考生在聽完題目後，需閱讀選項（CD不會播出），作一個正確回應選項的選擇。以下請聽CD練習30題模擬試題。

◆ 聽力測驗試題31～60題 🔘 5-02（請將答案寫在題號旁）

31. ＿＿＿＿＿＿＿＿＿＿＿＿＿＿＿＿＿＿＿＿＿

　　A. Yes, I'd like the number of Jane.

　　B. Yes, is that 222-5397?

　　C. Show me your phone number directly.

　　D. Sorry, I have little time.

32. ＿＿＿＿＿＿＿＿＿＿＿＿＿＿＿＿＿＿＿＿＿

　　A. Sure, let's go shopping.

　　B. I am afraid I can't. I have lots of assignments to do this afternoon.

　　C. I'm visiting your uncle, too.

　　D. Are you kidding me? No one will visit the Chen family.

33. ＿＿＿＿＿＿＿＿＿＿＿＿＿＿＿＿＿＿＿＿＿

　　A. Yes, I stayed there three nights.

　　B. Yes, she was. And she had a really great time there.

　　C. No, I wasn't. I had something else to do last night.

　　D. Alice is my best friend.

34. _____

    A. Well, I'll ask my academic advisor first.

    B. I'm running my business pretty well.

    C. No doubt. He wants to have history as my major.

    D. Frankly speaking, business in school is going down.

35. _____

    A. Yes, sir. May I help you?

    B. Yes, I think you're right about this.

    C. Do you have a driver's license?

    D. No problem. I'll take my coat and let's go!

36. _____

    A. Sure, please follow me.

    B. There is a window in the restaurant.

    C. The seat near windows is broken.

    D. I'm available.

37. _____

    A. He is like his brother.

    B. Yes, he is a little strict, though.

    C. I don't like my new classmate very much.

    D. I think he comes from Canada.

38. _____

    A. I am free now.

    B. It's ten past ten.

    C. I'll see you next time.

    D. I always study English when I have free time.

39. _____

    A. I don't like this movie.

    B. It's so kind of you to say that.

    C. I like all kinds of movies.

    D. My friends all like comedies.

40. _____

    A. It's about fifteen-minute walk.

    B. You're going too far.

    C. It's about three blocks from here to the bus station.

    D. In fact, it's about twenty kilograms.

41. _____

    A. Sure, please stand by me.

    B. Yes, there is one on the corner.

    C. Yes, I need some pills.

    D. Yes, there is a department store.

42. _____

    A. Maybe a necktie.

    B. Father's Day is on August 8th.

    C. Where is your father now?

    D. I will get a blade.

43. _____

    A. Her work starts at 9:00.

    B. I am sure that her idea will be very successful, too.

    C. Neither do I.

    D. Mary's idea is very honest, isn't it?

44. _____

    A. Then, we have to wait another 30 minutes.

    B. Does he take a school bus, too?

    C. The traffic is so heavy today.

    D. My God, who will drive me to school?

45. _____

    A. I played PC games yesterday.

    B. Ok, I am about to finish my homework.

    C. Give me ten more minutes, OK?

    D. It's high time to make your bed.

46. _____

    A. Just OK. Thanks a lot.

    B. Not everything, actually.

    C. From a point of view, it's not a good thing.

    D. They took a taxi.

47. _____

    A. Yes, that's a bad idea.

    B. Can you give me a hand?

    C. How many people will come here?

    D. No, that's really boring.

48. _____

    A. Why do you need me?

    B. I will go there immediately.

    C. Don't you need some stamps?

    D. Who needs to go there?

49. _____

    A. How do you do?

    B. I'm in the living room.

    C. I'm a translator.

    D. I am watching TV.

50. _____

    A. Raise the alarm in case of fire.

    B. You don't need to work today.

    C. Really? I will fix it.

    D. Why? I can't understand this lock.

51. _____

    A. Sure, that's your pen.

    B. That's OK. Just return it.

    C. Who made the mistake?

    D. That's OK. I think you took it on purpose.

52. _____

    A. No, but I am a computer expert.

    B. I think I couldn't use the computer when I was five.

    C. Yes, I've been using it for several years.

    D. The computer is so expensive.

53. _____

    A. Yes, there's a policeman directing traffic at the corner.

    B. There's a post office in the neighborhood.

    C. I saw you last night.

    D. No, he is not a policeman.

54. _____

    A. In the classroom.

    B. Right after school.

    C. Linda, her good friend.

    D. Do not talk now!

55. _____

    A. Why not have a cold drink and hide yourself in a cool room?

    B. Summer is also my favorite season.

    C. I am going swimming next summer.

    D. Yes, the hot pot is hotter and hotter.

56. _____

    A. I went dancing with my girlfriend.

    B. I'll call you back later.

    C. I am sorry, but you have the wrong number.

    D. I called on you yesterday.

57. _____

    A. I am on foot.

    B. I go to Taipei for work.

    C. I have been working in the same company for 3 years.

    D. I get along with my co-workers.

58. _____

    A. Yes, here you are.

    B. I can't offer you a special service.

    C. This is my last price.

    D. Yes, it is at the rock bottom price.

59. _____

    A. Yes, sir. May I help you?

    B. So am I.

    C. I couldn't agree with you.

    D. Yes, the restaurant is full of people.

60. _____

    A. Is it raining hard outside?

    B. We shall have a sunny weekend.

    C. You are always under the weather.

    D. Yes, you are completely right.

*問答題二解答請見第 188 頁。

■ 解答

◆ 問答題—聽力測驗試題敘述內容與解答1～30題

（C）1. The door has been open all day long.

　　　A. Yes, room 721.

　　　B. The store is closed.

　　　C. The house needs some fresh air.

（B）2. Who wants to play tennis?

　　　A. Yes, she is a tennis expert.

　　　B. I do.

　　　C. They want to play volleyball.

（A）3. Would you rather go jogging or take a walk?

　　　A. I really like walking.

　　　B. OK, that sounds nice.

　　　C. I walked the dog.

（B）4. Why is your hair wet?

　　　A. That's my hairnet.

　　　B. It's raining outside.

　　　C. You can take my umbrella.

（B）5. How many chairs do we need?

　　　A. These chairs are in order.

　　　B. We need at least 60.

　　　C. Our chairman is over 60.

（B）6. Whose brush is this?

　　　A. I lost my toothbrush.

　　　B. It's mine, but you can use it.

　　　C. Mr. Bush will be here soon.

（C）7. Which quarter are you taking Economics?

    A. My Economics professor did it.

    B. It's a half, not a quarter.

    C. Winter.

（C）8. You haven't signed the contract, have you?

    A. It's a contraction.

    B. No, the contractor is reputable.

    C. I did it last night.

（A）9. Does the rent include utilities?

    A. It includes everything except electricity.

    B. You could buy a heater.

    C. We are running out of gas.

（A）10. Whose name is the reservation under?

    A. It's under my father's name.

    B. It's under the chair.

    C. Let's make a reservation soon.

（C）11. Would you like to see my coin collection?

    A. She's a real collector.

    B. I'll correct your work in a while.

    C. Thanks, I'd enjoy that.

（B）12. Where will the new employee sit?

    A. The employer is in the board meeting.

    B. In the corner, I guess.

    C. The new employee has been retrenched.

(C) 13. Are you paying in cash or with a credit card?

    A. No, I don't have a check.

    B. I want to play cards.

    C. Credit card.

(C) 14. Could you cash the check in the bank?

    A. I don't know how to use a deposit slip.

    B. Of course, I did a thorough check already.

    C. No problem, I'll do it later.

(C) 15. Can you give me a cup of coffee?

    A. I don't know how to make the copy.

    B. I don't drink coffee.

    C. No problem. Cream and sugar?

(A) 16. Where is the nearest post office?

    A. Across from the street.

    B. In two days.

    C. By bus.

(A) 17. Has the architect visited you yet?

    A. Yes, we met the other day.

    B. Yes, I went there with the architect.

    C. Yes, the architect is looking at it.

(B) 18. Please give me the files on the merger.

    A. The merger is a big success.

    B. I'll have them ready for you in a while.

    C. The filing manager is exceptional.

（B）19. Who is your supervisor?

        A. They supervise me.

        B. Mr. White is.

        C. My supervisor is retiring next month.

（C）20. How much is the bus fare?

        A. The trade fair is well-attended.

        B. The bus stops here.

        C. Only 25 cents.

（A）21. Would you send the letter by overnight service?

        A. I mailed the letter just now.

        B. No, overnight service isn't expensive.

        C. OK. I'll do it later.

（B）22. I finally have my dental appointment.

        A. He is the best dentist in town.

        B. What's wrong with your teeth?

        C. I'm also very disappointed.

（C）23. Can we finish the project by the end of the week?

        A. Yes, our projection is right.

        B. Yes, the fiscal year ended last week.

        C. Not unless we hire more workers.

（C）24. When will we hear from the new client?

        A. Mr. Johnson is my client.

        B. You can use your mobile phone.

        C. After their meeting next Monday.

(C) 25. How long have you been working here?

  A. Since I am so busy.

  B. Not until 5:30.

  C. For 2 weeks now.

(B) 26. What is good for dessert in this restaurant?

  A. I recommend chicken for the main dish.

  B. Ice cream.

  C. The waiter deserted us.

(B) 27. Will the new ship sail soon?

  A. Yes, everything is on sale.

  B. Yes, it'll sail next week.

  C. In 5 days.

(A) 28. Why aren't these directors taking the subway?

  A. There's a delay on the tracks.

  B. Please show the directory.

  C. It's raining. Let's take a cab.

(C) 29. Excuse me, do you know if there's a grocery store nearby?

  A. You are excused.

  B. No, the stationery store is in the neighborhood.

  C. There are only some office buildings around here.

(A) 30. What is his idea for our print advertising?

  A. He said it depended on which newspaper would run our ads.

  B. He said he would print it out this afternoon.

  C. He said our competitors couldn't reach the right market.

◆問答題─聽力測驗試題中文翻譯1～30題

1. 門已經開了一整天了。
   A. 是的，721號房。
   B. 商店打烊了。
   C. 這房子需要一些新鮮空氣。

2. 誰想要打網球？
   A. 是的，她是網球專家。
   B. 我要。
   C. 他們想要打排球。

3. 你想要慢跑或是散路？
   A. 我真的較喜歡走路。
   B. 好的，那是個好主意。
   C. 我遛狗。

4. 為何你的頭髮是溼的？
   A. 那是我的網帽。
   B. 外面正在下雨。
   C. 你可以拿我的雨傘。

5. 我們需要幾張椅子？
   A. 這些椅子依序排好。
   B. 我們需要至少六十張。
   C. 我們的董事長超過六十歲。

6. 這是誰的刷子?
   A. 我失去我的牙刷。
   B. 是我的，但是你可以使用。
   C. 布希先生很快就會到。

7. 哪個學期你有修經濟學？
   A. 我經濟學教授做的。
   B. 這是一半，不是四分之一。
   C. 冬季。

8. 你尚未簽合約，不是嗎？
   A. 這是一個縮寫。
   B. 不，承包商是很有名聲的。
   C. 我昨晚簽了。

9. 租金有包含水電瓦斯嗎？
   A. 除了電費其他都有。
   B. 你可以買一個暖氣。
   C. 我們汽油快用完了。

10. 以誰的名義預約的？
    A. 以我父親的名義預約的。
    B. 在椅子底下。
    C. 讓我們快預約吧！

11. 你想看看我收集的硬幣嗎？
    A. 她真是一個收藏家。
    B. 我會很快修改你的作品。
    C. 謝謝，我很樂意。

12. 新來的員工要坐在哪兒？
    A. 雇主在開董事會。
    B. 我想在角落吧。
    C. 新員工已經被遣散了。

13. 你打算付現還是刷卡？
    A. 不，我沒有支票。
    B. 我想要玩牌。
    C. 信用卡。

14. 你可以到銀行兌現支票嗎？
    A. 我不知道如何使用存款單。
    B. 當然，我已經作了仔細的檢查。
    C. 沒問題，我待會做。

15. 可以給我一杯咖啡嗎？
    A. 我不知道如何影印。
    B. 我不喝咖啡。
    C. 沒問題。加奶精和糖嗎？

16. 最近的郵局在哪裡？
    A. 在對街。
    B. 再兩天。
    C. 搭公車。

17. 建築師有來見你嗎？
    A. 是的，我們幾天前見了。
    B. 是的，我與建築師到那裡。
    C. 是的，建築師正在看它。

18. 請給我有關併購的檔案。
    A. 併購案很成功。
    B. 我一會兒準備好給你。
    C. 檔案管理的經理很傑出。

19. 誰是你的主管？
    A. 他們管理監督我。
    B. 懷特先生。
    C. 我的主管下個月將退休。

20. 公車票多少錢？
    A. 貿易展人潮眾多。
    B. 這班公車停靠這裡。
    C. 只有25分錢。

21. 你想要用夜間郵寄的方式寄這封信嗎？
    A. 我剛才已經寄好了。
    B. 不，夜間郵寄不會很貴。
    C. 好，我待會會做。

22. 我終於完成牙醫的約診。
    A. 他是本地最棒的牙醫。
    B. 你的牙齒怎麼了？
    C. 我也失望。

23. 我們可以在本週末前完成計畫嗎？
    A. 是的，我們的預測是對的。
    B. 是的，財政年度上週結束。
    C. 除非我們僱用更多的員工才行。

24. 何時我們會有新客戶的消息？
    A. 強生先生是我的客戶。
    B. 你可以使用你的手機。
    C. 在他們下週一的會議之後。

25. 你在這裡工作多久了？
    A. 因爲我很忙。
    B. 要到五點半。
    C. 才兩週。

26. 這家餐廳的甜點哪個好？
    A. 主菜我推薦雞肉。
    B. 冰淇淋。
    C. 服務生遺棄我們。

27. 新船很快啟航嗎？
    A. 是的，所有的東西都特價。
    B. 是的，下週航行。
    C. 五天後。

28. 爲何這些主任不搭地鐵？
    A. 因爲火車有些延誤。
    B. 請把目錄秀出。
    C. 正在下雨。讓我們搭計程車吧。

29. 不好意思，你知道附近有超市嗎？
    A. 你被原諒了。
    B. 不，文具店在這個區域。
    C. 這附近只有一些辦公大樓。

30. 對我們的平面廣告，他的想法是？
    A. 他說要看是登在哪一家報紙而定。
    B. 他說他下午會印製出來。
    C. 他說我們的競爭者沒有達到正確的市場。

◆問答題二聽力測驗試題敘述內容與解答31～60題

（A）31. Directory assistance, may I help you?

    A. Yes, I'd like the number of Jane.

    B. Yes, is that 222-5397?

    C. Show me your phone number directly.

    D. Sorry, I have little time.

（B）32. I'm visiting Uncle Wang this afternoon. Are you coming with me?

    A. Sure, let's go shopping.

    B. I am afraid I can't. I have lots of assignments to do this afternoon.

    C. I'm visiting your uncle, too.

    D. Are you kidding me? No one will visit the Chen family.

（C）33. Weren't you at Alice's party last night?

    A. Yes, I stayed there three nights.

    B. Yes, she was. And she had a really great time there.

    C. No, I wasn't. I had something else to do last night.

    D. Alice is my best friend.

（A）34. Do you plan to major in business in college?

    A. Well, I'll ask my academic advisor first.

    B. I'm running my business pretty well.

    C. No doubt. He wants to have history as my major.

    D. Frankly speaking, business in school is going down.

（D）35. John, I am in a terrible hurry. Can you give me a ride?

    A. Yes, sir. May I help you?

    B. Yes, I think you're right about this.

    C. Do you have a driver's license?

    D. No problem. I'll take my coat and let's go!

（A）36. Is there a window seat available?

      A. Sure, please follow me.

      B. There is a window in the restaurant.

      C. The seat near windows is broken.

      D. I'm available.

（B）37. Do you like your new teacher, Chad?

      A. He is like his brother.

      B. Yes, he is a little strict, though.

      C. I don't like my new classmate very much.

      D. I think he comes from Canada.

（B）38. Do you have the time?

      A. I am free now.

      B. It's ten past ten.

      C. I'll see you next time.

      D. I always study English when I have free time.

（C）39. What kind of movies do you like?

      A. I don't like this movie.

      B. It's so kind of you to say that.

      C. I like all kinds of movies.

      D. My friends all like comedies.

（A）40. How far is the train station?

      A. It's about fifteen-minute walk.

      B. You're going too far.

      C. It's about three blocks from here to the bus station.

      D. In fact, It's about twenty kilograms.

（B）41. Is there a drugstore nearby?

    A. Sure, please stand by me.

    B. Yes, there is one on the corner.

    C. Yes, I need some pills.

    D. Yes, there is a department store.

（A）42. What are you going to buy for Father's Day?

    A. Maybe a necktie.

    B. Father's Day is on August 8th.

    C. Where is your father now?

    D. I will get a blade.

（C）43. To be honest, I don't think May's idea will work.

    A. Her work stats at 9:00.

    B. I am sure that her idea will be very successful, too.

    C. Neither do I.

    D. Mary's idea is very honest, isn't it?

（A）44. My heavens. The bus has just left.

    A. Then, we have to wait another 30 minutes.

    B. Does he take a school bus, too?

    C. The traffic is so heavy today.

    D. My God, who will drive me to school?

（C）45. Kenny, go to bed right now. You've been playing PC games for almost 3 hours.

    A. I played PC games yesterday.

    B. Ok, I am about to finish my homework.

    C. Give me ten more minutes, OK?

    D. It's high time to make your bed.

（A）46. How's everything going?

      A. Just OK. Thanks a lot.

      B. Not everything, actually.

      C. From a point of view, it's not a good thing.

      D. They took a taxi.

（D）47. Why not go for a picnic next time?

      A. Yes, that's a bad idea.

      B. Can you give me a hand?

      C. How many people will come here?

      D. No, that's really boring.

（B）48. Could you do me a favor? Go to the post office and buy some envelopes.

      A. Why do you need me?

      B. I will go there immediately.

      C. Don't you need some stamps?

      D. Who needs to go there?

（C）49. What do you do, Michelle?

      A. How do you do?

      B. I'm in the living room.

      C. I'm a translator.

      D. I am watching TV.

（C）50. My alarm clock didn't work today.

      A. Raise the alarm in case of fire.

      B. You don't need to work today.

      C. Really? I will fix it.

      D. Why? I can't understand this lock.

（B）51. I am sorry. I took your pen by mistake.

    A. Sure, that's your pen.

    B. That's OK. Just return it.

    C. Who made the mistake?

    D. That's OK.I think you took it on purpose.

（C）52. Can you use the computer, sir?

    A. No, but I am a computer expert.

    B. I think I couldn't use the computer when I was five.

    C. Yes, I've been using it for several years.

    D. The computer is so expensive.

（A）53. Excuse me, did you see a policeman nearby?

    A. Yes, there's a policeman directing traffic at the corner.

    B. There's a post office in the neighborhood.

    C. I saw you last night.

    D. No, he is not a policeman.

（C）54. Who's Jenny talking to now?

    A. In the classroom.

    B. Right after school.

    C. Linda, her good friend.

    D. Do not talk now!

（A）55. The weather's hotter and hotter. I hate summer.

    A. Why not have a cold drink and hide yourself in a cool room?

    B. Summer is also my favorite season.

    C. I am going swimming next summer.

    D. Yes, the hot pot is hotter and hotter.

（A）56. Where did you go last night? I called you several times, but I couldn't reach you.

    A. I went dancing with my girlfriend.

    B. I'll call back you later.

    C. I am sorry, but you have the wrong number.

    D. I called on you yesterday.

（A）57. How do you go to work every day?

    A. I am on foot.

    B. I go to Taipei for work.

    C. I have been working in the same company for 3 years.

    D. I get along with my co-workers.

（C）58. Could you give me a discount? I think it's too expensive.

    A. Yes, here you are.

    B. I can't offer you a special service.

    C. This is my last price.

    D. Yes, it is at the rock bottom price.

（B）59. I can't eat anymore. I am full.

    A. Yes, sir. May I help you?

    B. So am I.

    C. I couldn't agree with you.

    D. Yes, the restaurant is full of people.

（A）60. Oh, my shirt and pants are completely wet.

    A. Is it raining hard outside?

    B. We shall have a sunny weekend.

    C. You are always under the weather.

    D. Yes, you are completely right.

◆問答題二聽力測驗試題中文翻譯31～60題

31. 查號臺，我可以為你服務嗎？
    A.是的，我要珍的電話號碼。
    B.是的，那是222-5397嗎？
    C.直接告訴我你的電話號碼。
    D.抱歉，我沒有時間。

32. 我今午要去拜訪王叔叔，你要跟我一起來嗎？
    A.當然，讓我們一起去購物吧。
    B.恐怕不行，我下午還有許多未完成的工作要做。
    C.我也正要拜訪你的叔叔。
    D.你在開我玩笑嗎？沒有人將會拜訪陳家人。

33. 你昨晚沒在愛麗絲的派對裡嗎？
    A.是的，我在那裡三晚。
    B.是的，她是。而且她在那很愉快。
    C.不，我沒有。我昨晚有其他的事要做。
    D.愛麗絲是我最好的朋友。

34. 你大學計畫主修企管嗎？
    A.我將問問大學顧問。
    B.我經營我的事業相當不錯。
    C.不用懷疑的。他想以歷史做我的主修。
    D.坦白說學校的業務在下降中。

35. 約翰，我很匆忙，你可否載我一程？
    A.是的，我可以幫你嗎？
    B.我想你在這件事情上是對的。
    C.你有駕照嗎？
    D.沒問題，我拿件外套就走。

36. 有靠窗的位子嗎？
    A. 當然有，請隨我來。
    B. 有一個窗戶在這餐廳。
    C. 座位旁的窗戶壞了。
    D. 我有空。

37. 查德，你喜歡你的新老師嗎？
    A. 他像他的兄弟。
    B. 是的，雖然他有點嚴格。
    C. 我不是很喜歡我的新同學。
    D. 我想他是來自加拿大。

38. 現在幾點？
    A. 我現在有空。
    B. 十點過十分。
    C. 下回見。
    D. 我有空的時候總是讀英文。

39. 你喜歡何種電影？
    A. 我不喜歡這電影。
    B. 你人真好竟這麼說。
    C. 我喜歡所有種類的電影。
    D. 我的朋友都喜歡喜劇。

40. 火車站有多遠？
    A. 大約15分鐘路程。
    B. 你走太遠了。
    C. 從這裡到公車站大約三個街區距離。
    D. 事實上，它大概二十公斤。

41. 這附近有藥局嗎？
    A. 是的，請站在我旁邊。
    B. 是的，有一個就在角落。
    C. 是的，我需要一些藥丸。
    D. 是的，有一個百貨公司。

42. 你父親節將送什麼禮物？
    A. 也許是領帶吧。
    B. 父親節是8月8日。
    C. 你的父親在哪？
    D. 我將會得到一個刮鬍刀。

43. 老實說，我不認爲梅的想法可行。
    A. 她的工作九點開始。
    B. 我也認爲他的想法將會十分成功。
    C. 我也不認爲。
    D. 瑪麗的想法非常誠實，不是嗎？

44. 老天，公車剛跑掉。
    A. 那麼，我們要再等30分鐘。
    B. 他也搭校車嗎？
    C. 今天交通壅塞。
    D. 老天，誰要載我去學校？

45. 肯尼，趕快去睡覺，你已經玩電腦3個小時了。
    A. 我昨天玩電動。
    B. 好，我即將要完成我的作業。
    C. 再給我十分鐘好嗎？
    D. 是整理床鋪的時候了。

46. 一切都好吧？
    A. 還可以，謝謝。
    B. 事實上不是所有的事。
    C. 就我來看，這不是好事。
    D. 她們搭計程車。

47. 下回去野餐如何？
    A. 是的，那是個糟糕的主意。
    B. 你可以幫我嗎？
    C. 有幾個人會來？
    D. 不要，那實在很無聊。

48. 可否幫我一個忙，去郵局買一些信封袋。
    A. 為何你需要我？
    B. 我馬上去。
    C. 你難道不需要一些郵票？
    D. 誰需要去那裡？

49. 蜜雪兒，你的工作是？
    A. 你好嗎？
    B. 我在客廳裡。
    C. 我是翻譯人員。
    D. 我正在看電視。

50. 我的鬧鐘今天壞了。
    A. 失火時按警鈴。
    B. 你今天無須工作。
    C. 真的嗎，我來修理。
    D. 為何？我不懂這個鎖。

51. 很抱歉，我不小心拿了你的筆。
    A. 當然，那是你的筆。
    B. 沒關係，只要歸還即可。
    C. 誰犯錯？
    D. 沒關係。我想你是故意的。

52. 先生，你會操作電腦嗎？
    A. 不，但我是個電腦專家。
    B. 我想我五歲時不會打電腦。
    C. 是的，我使用電腦好多年了。
    D. 這電腦太貴了。

53. 對不起，你剛有看見警察在附近嗎？
    A. 是的，有個警察正在角落指揮交通。
    B. 附近有郵局。
    C. 我昨晚見到你。
    D. 不，他不是警察。

54. 珍妮正在和誰說話？
    A. 在教室。
    B. 就在放學後。
    C. 是琳達，她的好友。
    D. 現在別說話！

55. 天氣是越來越熱了。我真討厭夏天。
    A. 為何不來杯冷飲並把自己藏在涼快的房間裡？
    B. 夏季也是我最愛的季節。
    C. 我明年夏天將去游泳。
    D. 是的，熱鍋越來越熱。

56. 你昨天晚上去哪裡？我打幾次電話給你，但都找不到你。
    A. 我和女友去跳舞了。
    B. 我稍後回電。
    C. 抱歉你打錯電話。
    D. 我昨天拜訪你。

57. 你是如何去上班的？
    A. 走路去的。
    B. 我去臺北上班。
    C. 我已經在相同的公司工作三年了。
    D. 我與同事相處的好。

58. 你可以給我一個折扣嗎？這實在太貴了。
    A. 是的，在這裡。
    B. 我無法提供特別的服務。
    C. 這已經是最後底價了。
    D. 是的，這是超低價。

59. 我不能再吃了。
    A. 是的，我可以幫你嗎？
    B. 我也是。
    C. 我不能同意你的意見。
    D. 是，這餐廳充滿了人。

60. 噢，我的襯衫與長褲都溼透了。
    A. 外頭雨下很大嗎？
    B. 我們將有一個陽光的週末。
    C. 你總是不舒服。
    D. 是的，你對極了。

筆記頁

對話題

對話題的設計是在測驗考生對於英語對話的理解。在日常的生活中，英語的對話是包含談話者的表情、語氣、手勢與肢體動作（body language），我們可以由這些表現的輔助了解說話者所說的內容。但是在考試中，我們只能從說話者的語句、用字與語調來理解。所以這類的考題能測驗出考生對於英文字彙與慣用語的運用程度。幾乎所有的英語聽力考試均會有這樣的題型。托福（TOFEL）與雅思（IELTS）的考題為長篇的對話，而多益（TOEIC）、英檢（GEPT）以及高中英語聽力學測，則強調短篇的應對。

■ 本章重點

● 對話題一（ABA三段式對話）

● 對話題二（多段式對話）

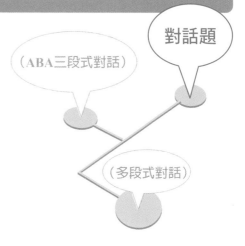

對話題

（ABA三段式對話）

（多段式對話）

● 對話題一（ABA三段式對話）

　　對話題一，設計的方式為A-B-A三段式的對應，一段對話配一題。其中對話與題目均由CD播出，選項則會出現在試題本上，考生需閱讀後再做四個選項的選擇。題目多以疑問詞（WH）的問句來問，除了對話中明確出現的資訊外，有時考題也會設計文中並未明確提到，而要考生推測的題目。例如有人提到I feel hungry.（我覺得餓）；考題就問出如Where might the woman go later?（這位女子待會可能去哪？）的題目，而考生就要選出如cafeteria（自助餐廳）或restaurant（餐廳）的選項。以下的二十組題目，就是以三段式的對話來出題。

◆ 聽力測驗試題1～20題，請聽CD完成以下20題模擬試題 6-01 。

1. _____

Q：Where are the speakers?

    A. At a shop.

    B. At a security checkpoint.

    C. In a theater.

    D. In a bank.

2. _____

Q：What is the man going to buy?

    A. The brown coat.

    B. The yellow coat.

    C. Both coats.

    D. The more expensive one.

3. _____

Q：How are they going to celebrate?

    A. Eat something.

    B. Play card games.

    C. Have some physical exams.

    D. Have a farewell party.

4. _____

Q：When is the flight?

    A. Two o'clock.

    B. Three o'clock.

    C. Four o'clock.

    D. Five o'clock.

5. _____

Q：Why can't the man get the monthly statement now?

    A. Because the woman is photocopying it.

    B. Because the woman is typing it.

    C. Because the woman is late for work.

    D. Because the statement is not clear.

6. _____

Q：What's wrong with the copy machine?

    A. No electricity.

    B. It's a brand new copy machine.

    C. Paper jams.

    D. The paper is too thin.

7. _____

Q：When is the show they're going to attend?

    A. One o'clock.

    B. Two o'clock.

    C. Four o'clock.

    D. Five o'clock.

8. _____

Q：What is the woman going to do?

    A. Find her wallet.

    B. Eat lunch.

    C. Lend $ 10 dollars.

    D. Take a bus home.

9. _____

Q：Where are the speakers?

    A. In a restaurant.

    B. In a baggage claim area.

    C. In a hotel.

    D. In a hearing.

10. _____

Q：What does the man want to find?

    A. Mail room.

    B. Security desk.

    C. Marketing department.

    D. Fire department.

11. _____

Q：Why do the speakers think Mary won't take this job offer?

    A. The pay is too low.

    B. The workload is too heavy.

    C. The location is inconvenient.

    D. The boss is too mean.

12. _____

Q：Where are the speakers going to celebrate this party?

    A. In a restaurant.

    B. In the main office.

    C. In the company cafeteria.

    D. In Italy.

13. _____

Q：What are the speakers talking about?

    A. How to evade getting fired.

    B. Start their own consulting firm.

    C. Today's news.

    D. Their ex-colleague's new job.

14. _____

Q：Where are the speakers?

    A. In a restroom.

    B. In a bookstore.

    C. In a hotel.

    D. In the city hall.

15. _____

Q：Why has the HR department been working hard lately?

    A. They have to do the final test for the new system.

    B. They have to make a presentation.

    C. They have to become board members.

    D. They have to do the payroll.

16. _____

Q：When does the work have to be done?

    A. Tomorrow.

    B. When the staff members from general affairs come.

    C. By Tuesday.

    D. By Thursday.

17. _____

Q：Why can't the man talk to his supervisor?

　　A. His supervisor tries to ignore him.

　　B. His supervisor doesn't open for advice.

　　C. His supervisor is too lazy.

　　D. His supervisor is so busy that he's got no time.

18. _____

Q：How does the woman feel about her current job?

　　A. Pleased.

　　B. Not pleased.

　　C. Excited.

　　D. Nervous.

19. _____

Q：What is the purpose of the party?

　　A. Graduation.

　　B. The year-end banquet.

　　C. Farewell.

　　D. Honor the most exceptional employee of this year.

20. _____

Q：What are they talking about?

　　A. Company event.

　　B. Family reunion.

　　C. Weather phenomenon.

　　D. Saturday's time sheets.

＊對話題一1-20題解答請見 212 頁

對話題二（多段式對話）

　　對話題二，設計的方式為A-B-A-B四段式的對應或是多段式的應對，一段對話配一題或是多題（即不只一題）。其中對話與題目均由CD播出，題目與選項則會出現在試題本上，考生需閱讀後再做四個選項的選擇。題目一樣多以疑問詞（WH）的問句來問。只是因為對話的字數變長，考生必須要更有耐心的將對話的內容聽完。

◆ 聽力測驗試題21～40題，請聽CD完成以下20題模擬試題 6-02

Q21 and 22 are according to the following conversation.

Q21: Where will the speakers probably eat on Sunday?

　　A. At a fast-food store.

　　B. Steak house.

　　C. Korean food restaurant.

　　D. Hotpot place.

Q22: What will the man do?

　　A. Call the restaurant.

　　B. Contact John.

　　C. Buy a pot.

　　D. Stay home on Sunday.

Q23 and 24 are according to the following conversation.

Q23: Where might the conversation take place?

　　A. In a company.

　　B. In the restaurant.

　　C. In the hospital.

　　D. In the hotel.

Q24: What does the woman ask for?

    A. A pen.

    B. A form.

    C. A minute.

    D. A chair.

Q25and 26 are according to the following conversation.

Q25: Which statement is true?

    A. The professor uses totally English in class.

    B. The speakers are high school students.

    C. The woman is worried about her "sociology".

    D. The professor doesn't give students too much homework.

Q26: Which subject is probably taught by the professor?

    A. Chinese.

    B. Sociology.

    C. English.

    D. Design.

Q27 is according to the following conversation.

Q27: Why does the woman want to give a gift to her teacher?

    A. Because tomorrow is Teacher's Day.

    B. Because her math teacher teaches well, and she wants to thank her.

    C. Because her math teacher is leaving next month.

    D. Because her math grades are improving a lot.

Q28 is according to the following conversation.

Q28: Which statement is true?

    A. It was a pity that the woman didn't come to the party.

B. The woman thought it was better to stay home last night.

C. The man invites the woman to the next party.

D. The woman feels sorry that she went to the party last night.

Q29 is according to the following conversatuion.

Q29: Which statement is "Not" true?

A. Chris's phone number is 2355-4562.

B. Mary is out for business.

C. Chris leaves Mary a message.

D. The man wants to talk to Mary.

Q30 and 31 are according to the following conversation.

Q30: When did the woman buy these sandals?

A. She bought them last weekend.

B. She bought them when the department store had a big sale.

C. When her friend came.

D. When she was on vacation.

Q31: How much are these sandals?

A. $19.

B. $15.

C. $30.

D. $60.

Q32 and 33 are according to the following conversation.

Q32: Where is Nick?

A. At the supermarket.

B. At dessert house.

C. At home.

D. Outside.

Q33: Which statement is true?

    A. Nick is at the supermarket now.

    B. Nick needs some orange juice, bread and eggs.

    C. The woman wants to know what Nick needs.

    D. The woman thinks desserts are not good for the man.

Q34 is according to the following conversation.

Q34: Why does the woman say "wait a second"?

    A. Because she is wondering if the man has been accepted by Hawaii University.

    B. Because she is wondering what the purpose of the man's trip is.

    C. Because she is lying on the beach.

    D. Because the woman wants to have a vacation too.

Q35 and 36 are according to the following conversation.

Q35: Do they have sandwiches at their picnic in the end?

    A. Sure, and they also bring some salad.

    B. No, but they will take them next time.

    C. No, and the man will go to the traditional market to buy other things.

    D. They want to have something different.

Q36: What will the woman do now?

    A. Make dinner.

    B. Make a phone call.

    C. Go to the supermarket.

    D. Eat salad.

Q37 is according to the following conversation.

Q37: Why did the man hurt his leg?

A. Because he played baseball.

B. Because he played basketball.

C. Because he tripped at home.

D. Because he had a trip yesterday.

Q38 is according to the following conversation.

Q38: What happened to the little girl?

A. She won a swimming race.

B. She pushed someone into the pool.

C. She was pushed into the swimming pool.

D. She reported the accident.

Q39 is according to the following conversation.

Q39: Why can't the man see the movie on Friday night?

A. The movie doesn't show on Friday.

B. Friday is not a holiday.

C. There are no available tickets left.

D. It's too late to order tickets.

Q40 is according to the following conversation.

Q40: What are the speakers going to do later?

A. Use the computer.

B. Go downtown.

C. Answer many email messages.

D. Eat lunch.

*對話題二21-40題解答請見 226 頁。

■ 解答

◆ 對話題—聽力測驗試題敘述內容與解答1～20題

1. M: May I see your receipt?

W: Here it is. I just paid at Aisle seven.

M: OK, please take this to the cashier to get the tag removed.

（A）Q: Where are the speakers?

A. At a shop.

B. At a security checkpoint.

C. In a theater.

D. In a bank.

2. M: This brown coat is $20.

W: That's twice as much as the other yellow one.

M: I'll buy the cheaper one. That'll be a right decision.

（B）Q: What is the man going to buy?

A. The brown coat.

B. The yellow coat.

C. Both coats.

D. The more expensive one.

3. M: I passed the final exam.

W: Congratulations. So did I.

M: Let's go celebrate and have a big meal.

（A）Q: How are they going to celebrate?

A. Eat something.

B. Play card games.

C. Have some physical exams.

D. Have a farewell party.

4. M: I can get you on the 5 o'clock flight.

　　W: Fine. Can I have an aisle seat please?

　　M: Sorry. There are only window seats left.

　（D）Q: When is the flight?

　　　　　A. Two o'clock.

　　　　　B. Three o'clock.

　　　　　C. Four o'clock.

　　　　　D. Five o'clock.

5. M: Do you have the latest monthly statement?

　　W: I am typing it right now.

　　M: Please give me one copy when you are done.

　（B）Q: Why can't the man get the monthly statement now?

　　　　　A. Because the woman is photocopying it.

　　　　　B. Because the woman is typing it.

　　　　　C. Because the woman is late for work.

　　　　　D. Because the statement is not clear.

6. M: The paper jams in this copier.

　　W: This is the fifth time this week. I say we buy a brand new one.

　　M: You are right. I'll make a phone call later.

　（C）Q: What's wrong with the copy machine?

　　　　　A. No electricity.

　　　　　B. It's a brand new copy machine.

　　　　　C. Paper jams.

　　　　　D. The paper is too thin.

7. M: When does the cooking demonstration start?

W: There are two shows. One is at four and one at five.

M: Let's go to the earlier one!

（C） Q: When is the show they're going to attend?

A. One o'clock.

B. Two o'clock.

C. Four o'clock.

D. Five o'clock.

8. M: What's wrong?

W: I can't find my wallet. I must have left it on the bus when I came here. Now I have no money to buy my lunch.

M: Here's $10. Take it!

（B） Q: What is the woman going to do?

A. Find her wallet.

B. Eat lunch.

C. Lend $ 10 dollars.

D. Take a bus home.

9. M: Where is our waitress?

W: We've been waiting here for at least 20 minutes.

M: I'll never come here again!

（A） Q: Where are the speakers?

A. In a restaurant.

B. In a baggage claim area.

C. In a hotel.

D. In a hearing.

10. M: How can I get to the marketing department?

W: Go straight and pass the mail room. Turn right at the security desk.

M: Thank you. I can find it.

（C）Q: What does the man want to find?

    A. Mail room.

    B. Security desk.

    C. Marketing department.

    D. Fire department.

11. M: The job description calls for twice as much work at the same salary and benefits Mary has now.

W: So I guess she won't take this job offer.

M: Not that I know of.

（A）Q: Why do the speakers think Mary won't take this job offer?

    A. The pay is too low.

    B. The workload is too heavy.

    C. The location is inconvenient.

    D. The boss is too mean.

12. M: Let's have Mr. Cho's retirement party in the main office.

W: I don't think it can hold so many people there. Let's have it in the company cafeteria.

M: No, the cafeteria is being remodeled now. I'll call that Italian restaurant around the corner from here.

（A）Q: Where are the speakers going to celebrate this party?

    A. In a restaurant.

    B. In the main office.

C. In the company cafeteria.

D. In Italy.

13. M: Did you have news about Charles Wang?

    W: You mean that he got fired and then started his own consulting firm down the street?

    M: That's right. I wonder how he's working without our company.

（D）Q: What are the speakers talking about?

       A. How to evade getting fired.

       B. Start their own consulting firm.

       C. Today's news.

       D. Their ex-colleague's new job.

14. W: I am sorry, sir. We're completely booked tonight. There are no rooms available until the day after tomorrow.

    M: I see. Is there someplace nearby you recommend I might be able to stay?

    W: Here's the city map. There are some other hotels in this area.

（C）Q: Where are the speakers?

       A. In a restroom.

       B. In a bookstore.

       C. In a hotel.

       D. In the city hall.

15. M: The HR department has been working so hard these days.

    W: I know. They've even been in the office on weekends. Do you think they'll be ready to make the presentation to the board members?

    M: That's for sure! They will make their final revisions soon.

（B）Q: Why has the HR department been working hard lately?

    A. They have to do the final test for the new system.

    B. They have to make a presentation.

    C. They have to become board members.

    D. They have to do the payroll.

16. M: We have to get this work done by Thursday.

    W: I can't do it unless I have more help.

    M: I'll ask some staff members from general affairs to help you, or maybe tomorrow you can hire as many temporary workers as you need.

（D）Q: When does the work have to be done?

    A. Tomorrow.

    B. When the staff members from general affairs come.

    C. By Tuesday.

    D. By Thursday.

17. M: Have you given your advice to your supervisor yet?

    W: No, he's always too busy with something else.

    M: He never makes time for his staff, even a minute.

（D）Q: Why can't the man talk to his supervisor?

    A. His supervisor tries to ignore him.

    B. His supervisor doesn't open for advice.

    C. His supervisor is too lazy.

    D. His supervisor is so busy that he's got no time.

18. W: I think I should start looking for another job.

    M: I thought you are happy with your present one.

    W: I used to be, but after the promotion, I didn't get a raise.

（B）Q: How does the woman feel about her current job?

    A. Pleased.

     B. Not pleased.

    C. Excited.

    D. Nervous.

19. M: Did you know that tomorrow evening's farewell party for Dr. Chen has been postponed?

   W: Yes, I was told this morning they've rescheduled it for the beginning of next month.

   M: I'm afraid I can't attend then.

（C）Q: What is the purpose of the party?

    A. Graduation.

    B. The year-end banquet.

    C. Farewell.

    D. Honor the most exceptional employee of this year.

20. M: Did you remember that we're having a company outing this weekend?

   W: I did, but the weather forecast for Saturday isn't very good. Is there a rain date?

   M: It's the following Saturday.

（A）Q: What are they talking about?

    A. Company event.

    B. Family reunion.

    C. Weather phenomenon.

    D. Saturday's time sheets.

◆ 對話題一聽力測驗試題中文翻譯1～20題

1. W：先生，我可以看你的收據嗎？
   M：在這裡。我剛在第七道付款。
   W：好的，請把這個拿給出納員移除這個標籤。

   Q：說話者現在人在何處？
   　　A. 商店中。
   　　B. 安檢關卡。
   　　C. 戲院。
   　　D. 銀行。

2. M：這件咖啡色外套二十元。
   W：那是黃色那件的兩倍。
   M：我想我會買較便宜的那一件。那將是正確的決定。

   Q：男子將會買哪一件？
   　　A. 咖啡色外套。
   　　B. 黃色外套。
   　　C. 兩件外套。
   　　D. 較貴的那一件。

3. M：我通過了期末考。
   W：恭喜！我也是。
   M：我們去慶祝一下，吃頓大餐吧。

   Q：他們將如何慶祝？
   　　A. 吃一些東西。
   　　B. 玩牌。
   　　C. 作身體健檢。
   　　D. 開歡送派對。

4. M：我可以讓你坐五點的班機。

　　W：很好。可否給我靠走道的座位？

　　M：很抱歉。只剩下靠窗的座位了。

　　Q：班機的時間是幾點？

　　　　A. 兩點鐘。

　　　　B. 三點鐘。

　　　　C. 四點鐘。

　　　　D. 五點鐘。

5. M：你有最新的月報表嗎？

　　W：我現在正在打。

　　M：完成後請給我一份。

　　Q：為何男士目前無法拿到月報表？

　　　　A. 因為女士正在拷貝。

　　　　B. 因為女士正在打字。

　　　　C. 因為女士上班遲到。

　　　　D. 因為報表不清楚。

6. M：影印機卡紙了。

　　W：這是本週的第五回了。我認為我們應該立即買一臺新的。

　　M：你說的對。我待會來打電話。

　　Q：影印機怎麼了？

　　　　A. 沒電。

　　　　B. 它是一個全新的影印機。

　　　　C. 卡紙。

　　　　D. 影印紙太薄了。

7. M：烹飪展何時開始？

　W：有兩場秀。一場在四點，一場在五點。

　M：我們去較早的那一場！

　Q：他們要看哪一場表演？
　　　A. 一點鐘。
　　　B. 兩點鐘。
　　　C. 四點鐘。
　　　D. 五點鐘。

8. M：怎麼了？

　W：我找不到我的皮夾。我一定是在我來這裡時，把它遺留在公車上。現在我沒錢買午餐了。

　M：這裡有十元。你拿去吧！

　Q：女士將要作什麼？
　　　A. 找她的皮夾。
　　　B. 吃午餐。
　　　C. 借出十元。
　　　D. 搭公車回家。

9. M：我們的服務生呢？

　W：我們已經在這裡等了至少二十分鐘了。

　M：我再也不會來了！

　Q：說話者人在哪裡？
　　　A. 餐廳。
　　　B. 行李認領處。
　　　C. 飯店。
　　　D. 公聽會。

10.M：行銷部門要怎麼去？

W：直走並通過郵件收發室。在服務臺的地方再向右轉。

M：謝謝。我找得到。

Q：這男人想要找什麼地方？

A. 郵件收發室。

B. 服務臺。

C. 行銷部門。

D. 消防局。

11.M：這個工作比瑪麗現有的工作量多兩倍，但卻給一樣的薪資與福利。

W：我想她不會接受這份工作。

M：據我所知不會。

Q：為何說話者認為瑪麗不會接受這份工作？

A. 薪資太低。

B. 工作量太重。

C. 位置不方便。

D. 老闆太壞。

12.M：讓我們在大辦公室舉行邱先生的退休派對吧。

W：我不認為那裡可以容納那麼多人。讓我們在公司餐廳辦吧。

M：不行，公司的餐廳現在在整修。我來打電話給轉角的那家義式料理店。

Q：說話者要在哪裡舉辦退休派對？

A. 餐廳。

B. 大辦公室。

C. 公司餐廳。

D. 義大利。

13.M：你知道查爾斯王的消息嗎？

W：你是說他被開除了，之後又在街底開了一間他自己的顧問公司。

M：對，我在想他沒有我們公司不知道做得如何？

Q：說話者在討論什麼？

A. 如何避免被開除。

B. 開始他們自己的顧問公司。

C. 今日的新聞。

D. 前同事的新工作。

14.W：先生不好意思，我們今晚的房間都訂滿了。到後天才會有房間。

M：了解。你能推薦附近有無其他的地方我可以住？

W：這是本市地圖。這個區域有其他的旅館。

Q：說話者人在何處？

A. 廁所。

B. 書店。

C. 旅館。

D. 市政府。

15.M：人事部門這幾天工作量都很大。

W：我知道。他們甚至週末都待在辦公室。你認為他們準備好給董事會的簡報嗎？

M：那是當然的。他們將會很快完成最後的修正。

Q：爲什麼最近人事部門工作繁重？
　　A. 他們要對新系統作最後的測試。
　　B. 他們要做簡報。
　　C. 他們要成爲董事會的成員。
　　D. 他們要做薪資條。

16.M：我們必須在週四前完成這份工作。
　　W：我沒辦法的，除非我有更多的協助。
　　M：我會請總務部門的人來幫你，或是也許明天你也可以僱
　　　　用你需要的臨時工。

　　Q：這份工作何時要完成？
　　　　A. 明天。
　　　　B. 當總務部門的人員來時。
　　　　C. 週二前。
　　　　D. 週四前。

17.M：你有把意見給你的主管了嗎？
　　W：沒有，他總是太忙而沒時間與別人討論事情。
　　M：他從不留時間給他的員工，甚至連一分鐘都不。

　　Q：爲什麼男士無法與他的主管說話？
　　　　A. 他的主管試著要忽視他。
　　　　B. 他的主管不接受建議。
　　　　C. 他的主管太懶。
　　　　D. 他的主管太忙沒空。

18.W：我想我應該要開始找新工作。
　　M：我以爲你對目前的工作很滿意。
　　W：以前是的。但在試用期過後，我沒有加薪。

Q：女士對她目前的工作感覺如何？
　　A. 高興。
　　B. 不高興。
　　C. 興奮。
　　D. 緊張。

19.M：你知道明晚爲陳醫生辦的歡送會延後了嗎？
　　W：我知道。我今早被告知他們將這個會改成下月初。
　　M：恐怕到那時我不能參加。

Q：這個派對的目的是？
　　A. 畢業。
　　B. 年終尾牙。
　　C. 歡送會。
　　D. 表揚年度最佳員工。

20.M：你記得我們本週末有公司旅遊嗎？
　　W：我記得，但是氣象預測說週六的天氣不是很好。有因爲
　　　　下雨而順延的日期嗎？
　　M：就是再下個週六。

Q：他們在討論什麼？
　　A. 公司活動。
　　B. 家庭聚會。
　　C. 大氣現象。
　　D. 週六的工時表。

◆ 對話題二聽力測驗試題敘述內容與解答21～40題

21 and 22

W: John was talking about going out to eat on Sunday. Maybe we'll go one of those hotpot places.

M: I have a better idea. Let's go for Korean food. I know one terrific restaurant.

W: Fine with me. But, I am not sure if John is OK.

M: Let me suggest it to John. I think that'd be fine with him, too.

W: Can you call him now?

（C）Q21: Where will the speakers probably eat on Sunday?

      A. At a fast-food store.

      B. In a steak house.

      C. In a korean food restaurant.

      D. At a hotpot place.

（B）Q22: What will the man do?

      A. Call the restaurant.

      B. Contact John.

      C. Buy a pot.

      D. Stay home on Sunday.

23 and 24

W: I am here for an interview. I've got an appointment with the marketing manager.

M: Please have a seat and fill out the form. And I'll have him talk to you in a few minutes.

W: Can I have a pen?

M: Sure. Here you are.

（A）Q23: Where might the conversation take place?

      A. In a company.

      B. In the restaurant.

      C. In the hospital.

      D. In the hotel.

（A）Q24: What does the woman ask for?

      A. A pen.

      B. A form.

      C. A minute.

      D. A chair.

25 and 26

W: Oh, I wish this sociology textbook wasn't so difficult. I can't believe all this new English vocabulary.

M: Take it easy. The professor will explain everything in Chinese.

W: OK.

M: But that's not so OK. The professor always assigns lots of homework.

W: What a busy college life!

（C）Q25: Which statement is true?

      A. The professor uses totally English in class.

      B. The speakers are high school students.

      C. The woman is worried about her "sociology".

      D. The professor doesn't give students too much homework.

（B）Q26: Which subject is probablytaught by the professor?

      A. Chinese.

      B. Sociology.

      C. English.

      D. Design.

27

W: I need to buy some presents for my teachers.

M: Why? Is it Teacher's Day tomorrow?

W: No, but I want to thank my math teacher because he teaches so well.

M: Oh, you are also a nice student.

（B）Q27: Why does the woman want to give a gift to her teacher?

      A. Because tomorrow is Teacher's Day.

      B. Because her math teacher teaches well, and she wants to thank her.

      C. Because her math teacher is leaving next month.

      D. Because her math grades are improving a lot.

28

W: I wish I had gone to your party last night.

M: Yes, why didn't you come? There was some music you love.

W: I know. If I hadn't needed to do homework, I would have come.

M: Here, let me show you some pictures of yesterday's party.

（A）Q28: Which statement is true?

      A. It was a pity that the woman didn't come to the party.

      B. The woman thought it was better to stay home last night.

      C. The man invites the woman to the next party.

      D. The woman feels sorry that she went to the party last night.

29

W: May I speak to Mary, please?

M: I'm sorry, she's out for lunch. Do you want to leave your message?

W: Oh, my name's Chris. My telephone number is 2355-4562.

M: Ok, I'll leave her the message.

（B）Q29: Which statement is "NOT" true?

    A. Chris's phone number is 2355-4562.

    B. Mary is out for business.

    C. Chris leaves Mary a message.

    D. The man wants to talk to Mary.

30 and 31

M: I haven't seen you wear those sandals before.

W: Oh, they are new.

M: Well, where did you buy them?

W: I bought them in the NY19 Department Store when it had a big sale.

M: How much are they?

W: Originally $30, but I got them for half price.

（B）Q30: When did the woman buy these sandals?

    A. She bought them last weekend.

    B. She bought them when the department store had a big sale.

    C. When her friend came.

    D. When she was on vacation.

（B）Q31: How much are these sandals?

    A. $19.

    B. $15.

    C. $30.

    D. $60.

32 and 33

W: Hello, Nick, I'm at the supermarket. What do you need at home?

M: Hi, we're out of milk, eggs, and orange juice in the refrigerator.

W: How about cake and chips?

M: Don't eat too many desserts. They are not good for you.

（C）Q32: Where is Nick?

　　　　A. At the supermarket.

　　　　B. At dessert house.

　　　　C. At home.

　　　　D. Outside.

（C）Q33: Which statement is true?

　　　　A. Nick is at the supermarket now.

　　　　B. Nick needs some orange juice, bread and eggs.

　　　　C. The woman wants to know what Nick needs.

　　　　D. The woman thinks desserts are not good for the man.

34

W: I heard you were accepted at the University of Hawaii.

M: Yes, I'm looking forward to lying on the sandy beach and watching hot girls.

W: Wait a second. Will you go to study or vacation?

M: We have to cherish our lives, you know.

（B）Q34: Why does the woman say "wait a second"?

　　　　A. Because she is wondering if the man has been accepted by Hawaii University.

　　　　B. Because she is wondering what the purpose of the man's trip is.

　　　　C. Because she is lying on the beach.

　　　　D. Because the woman wants to have a vacation too.

35 and 36

W: What are we having at picnic, Bill? I am definitely tired of sandwiches again.

M: Let's have salad instead.

W: I don't think that's enough. We have 5 people in total.

M: OK, OK. I think I'll go around the supermarket, and try to find something we can eat for picnic.

W: Meanwhile, I'll call the people to remind them.

（D）Q35: Do they have sandwiches at their picnic in the end?

      A. Sure, and they also bring some salad.

      B. No, but they will take them next time.

      C. No, and the man will go to the traditional market to buy other things.

      D. No, because they want to have something different.

（B）Q36: What will the woman do now?

      A. Make dinner.

      B. Make phone calls.

      C. Go to the supermarket.

      D. Eat salad.

37

W: Don't tell me you hurt your leg playing basketball again!

M: Actually, I tripped on the rug in my living room yesterday.

W: I hope you will recover in time to play on your baseball team Sunday afternoon.

M: Thank you.

（C）Q37: Why did the man hurt his leg?

      A. Because he played baseball.

      B. Because he played basketball.

      C. Because he tripped at home.

      D. Because he had a trip yesterday.

38

W: Someone pushed the little girl into the pool.

M: Did they push her on purpose?

W: I don't think so.

M: Why was that?

W: It was just an accident. Luckily, the girl can swim.

（C）Q38: What happened to the little girl?

      A. She won the swimming race.

      B. She pushed someone into the pool.

      C. She was pushed into the swimming pool.

      D. She reported the accident.

39

M: I need to call the box to order some Thursday's movie tickets.

W: Why don't you see the movie this Friday night?

M: It shows only Monday through Thursday.

W: OK.

（A）Q39: Why can't the man see the movie on Friday night?

      A. The movie doesn't show on Friday.

      B. Friday is not a holiday.

      C. There are no available tickets left.

      D. It's too late to order tickets.

40

M: You've been using your computer all morning. Why don't you take a break?

W: I have lots of email messages to answer.

M: Well, it's lunchtime. Let's go out to eat. I am starving!

W: You go ahead, and I'll meet you at the café downstairs in ten minutes.

（D）Q40: What are the speakers going to do later?

　　　　A. Use the computer.

　　　　B. Go downtown.

　　　　C. Answer many email messages.

　　　　D. Eat lunch.

◆ 對話題二聽力測驗試題中文翻譯21～40題

21與22題

女：約翰討論著週日去外面吃。也許我們會去一家火鍋店。

男：我有一個更好的主意。讓我們吃韓國餐吧。我知道一家很棒的餐廳。

女：我可以。但是我不確定約翰是否可以。

男：讓我來建議約翰。我想對他來說應該也沒問題。

女：你現在可以打電話給他嗎？

Q21：說話者星期天可能要去吃什麼？

    A. 速食。

    B. 牛排館。

    C. 韓國餐館。

    D. 火鍋。

Q22：男士將要作什麼？

    A. 打電話給餐廳。

    B. 聯絡約翰。

    C. 買鍋子。

    D. 週日時待在家裡。

23與24題

女：我是來面試的。我與行銷經理有約。

男：請坐，並把這表格填好。我幾分鐘後請他再與你談。

女：可以借支筆嗎？

男：沒問題，給你。

Q23：這對話的發生地是？

    A. 在一家公司。

    B. 在餐館。

　　　　C. 在醫院。
　　　　D. 在旅館。

Q24：這女子要什麼？
　　　　A. 一支筆。
　　　　B. 一張表格。
　　　　C. 一分鐘。
　　　　D. 一張椅子。

25與26題

女：噢，我希望這社會學課本不這麼難。我不敢相信都是新的
　　英文單字。
男：放輕鬆。教授會用中文解釋內容。
女：好吧。
男：沒那麼好。這教授總是給我們很多作業。
女：多忙碌的大學生活呀！

Q25：哪一項說法是正確的？
　　　　A. 教授用全英文教學。
　　　　B. 說話者是高中生。
　　　　C. 這女人擔心她的社會學科。
　　　　D. 這教授不會給太多的作業。

Q26：哪一個科目被這位教授指導？
　　　　A. 中文。
　　　　B. 社會學。
　　　　C. 英文。
　　　　D. 設計。

27題

女：我需要買一些禮物給我的老師。

男：爲什麼？明天是教師節嗎？

女：不是，但是我想要謝謝我的數學老師因爲他教太好了。

男：噢，我想你也是一位好學生。

Q27：爲何這女人要給她的老師禮物？

　　A. 因爲明天是教師節了。

　　B. 因爲她的數學老師教的好，她想要謝謝她。

　　C. 因爲她的數學老師下個月將離去。

　　D. 因爲她的數學成績進步很多。

28題

女：我希望我昨晚有去你的宴會。

男：對呀，你爲何沒有來？好多的音樂是你喜歡的。

女：我知道，假如我不需要寫作業的話，我就會來了。

男：嘿，讓我秀給你看一些昨日派對的照片。

Q28：哪一個是眞的？

　　A. 那女人沒參加派對是件可惜的事。

　　B. 這女人認爲昨晚最好待在家中。

　　C. 這男人邀請女人到下一場的派對。

　　D. 這女人對於她昨晚去的這個派對感到難過。

29題

女：我可以和瑪麗說話嗎？

男：抱歉，她外出吃飯。你要留言嗎？

女：噢，我的名字是克里斯。我的電話號碼是2355-4562。

男：沒問題，我會給她這個訊息。

Q29：哪一個敘述不真？

    A. 克里斯的電話號碼是2355-4562。

    B. 瑪麗外出洽公。

    C. 克里斯留給瑪麗一個訊息。

    D. 這位男士想要與瑪麗說話。

30與31題

男：我以前沒看過你穿這涼鞋。

女：是的，它們是新的。

男：噢，你在哪兒買的？

女：我在NY19百貨公司有特價時買的。

男：多少錢啊？

女：原價30元，但是我是用半價買的。

Q30：這女士何時買了涼鞋？

    A. 她在上週末買的。

    B. 她在當百貨公司大減價時買的。

    C. 當她朋友來時。

    D. 當她度假時。

Q31：這雙涼鞋多少錢？

    A. $19。

    B. $15。

    C. $30。

    D. $60。

32與33題

女：嗨，尼克，我在超市。你要不要什麼東西？

男：嗨，我們冰箱裡沒有牛奶、雞蛋與柳丁汁。

女：蛋糕與洋芋片呢？

男：別吃太多的甜點。那對你身體不好。

Q32：尼克在哪裡？

    A. 在超市。

    B. 在甜點屋。

    C. 在家裡。

    D. 在外頭。

Q33：哪一個說法是正確的？

    A. 尼克正在超市。

    B. 尼克需要一些柳丁汁，麵包與雞蛋。

    C. 這女士想知道尼克要什麼。

    D. 這女士認爲甜點對這男子不好。

34題

女：我聽說你被夏威夷大學接受入學許可了。

男：是的，我期待躺在沙灘上並看性感的女子。

女：等一下，你是要去讀書還是度假？

男：你知道的，我們必須珍惜我們的人生。

Q34：這女士爲何說「稍等一下」？

    A. 因爲她懷疑是否這男人已經被夏威夷大學接受了。

    B. 因爲她在想這男士這趟行程的目的爲何。

    C. 因爲她正躺在沙灘上。

    D. 因爲這女人也想要有一個假期。

35與36題

女：比爾，野餐吃什麼？我眞的厭倦了又吃三明治。

男：讓我們改吃沙拉吧。

女：我想那不夠吃。我們一共有五人。

男：好吧好吧，我會去一趟超市，試著找一些我們野餐可以吃
　　的東西。

女：同時，我也來打電話提醒他們。

Q35：他們最後吃三明治嗎？

　　A. 是，他們也會帶一些沙拉。

　　B. 不，但是他們將會下次帶。

　　C. 不，這男人將會去傳統市場再買一些其他的東西。

　　D. 不，他們想換不一樣的東西。

Q36：女士接下來要做什麼？

　　A. 煮晚餐。

　　B. 打電話。

　　C. 去超市。

　　D. 吃沙拉。

37題

女：別告訴我你又打籃球傷了你的腿。

男：事實上，我是在昨天被我客廳裡的地毯絆倒。

女：我希望你趕快康復，就可以打週日下午的棒球賽。

男：謝謝。

Q37：爲何男士的腿受傷了？

　　A. 因爲他打棒球。

　　B. 因爲他打籃球。

　　C. 因爲他在家裡絆倒了。

　　D. 因爲他昨日有旅行。

38題

女：有人把小女孩推入泳池。

男：是故意的嗎？

女：我想不是。

男：那是爲什麼？

女：這只是一個意外。幸運地，這女孩會游泳。

Q38：這小女孩怎麼了？

    A. 她贏得游泳比賽。

    B. 她推人至泳池。

    C. 她被人推入泳池。

    D. 她報案了。

39題

男：我需要打個電話來訂週四的電影票。

女：我們為何不在週五晚看電影？

男：這部片只有週一到週四上映。

女：好吧。

Q39：為何他們不在週五晚看電影？

    A. 這部電影週五沒有上映。

    B. 週五不是假日。

    C. 沒有剩票了。

    D. 太晚了無法訂票。

40題

男：你整個早上都在用電腦。為何不休息一下？

女：我有很多的電子郵件訊息要回。

男：嗯，現在是午餐時間。我們外出吃飯吧。我餓死了！

女：你先去，我十分鐘後跟你在樓下的咖啡廳見。

Q40：說話者接下來要做什麼？

    A. 用電腦。

    B. 去市中心。

    C. 回覆很多電子郵件訊息。

    D. 吃午餐。

7 短文獨白題

短文獨白題的設計是在考考生對於英語談話的理解度。所以這類的考題能考出考生對於說話者所談之內容的理解程度（Listening Comprehension）。一般留學的英文聽力考試均會有這樣的題型。這類題型的主題十分多樣化，舉凡車站或是機場的廣播，課堂上的授課或演說，以及新聞或氣象的報導等，能夠真正測出學生的英文聽力的能力。

■ 本章重點

● 短文獨白題一（一段對應一題）
● 短文獨白題二（一段對應三題）

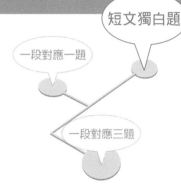

短文獨白題
一段對應一題
一段對應三題

● 短文獨白題一（一段對應一題）

　　短文獨白題一，設計的方式為一段式的談話，搭配一個問題。其中談話均由CD播出，題目的選項則會出現在試題本上，考生需閱讀後再做四個選項的選擇。題目以疑問詞（WH）的問句來問，也就是要考生能辨別時間，辨別地點，辨別原因，辨別人物以及辨別意圖等能力。此種題目的作答方式，一定要先看題目，辨別所問問題的目的與方向，並注意相關關鍵字，再刪除多餘的聽力障礙字後，便可以輕鬆得分。

◆ 聽力測驗試題1～10題，請聽CD完成以下10題模擬試題，並將答案寫在題號旁 🔵 7-01。

1. _____

Q：What happens if a customer presses 2?

    A. The customer can talk to the customer service.

    B. The customer can order something.

    C. The customer can get information about return policy.

    D. The customer can get the money back.

2. _____

Q：What is the relationship between the speaker and John?

    A. Manager and staff.

    B. Teacher and student.

    C. Parent and child.

    D. Husband and wife.

3. _____

Q：When can people listen to a speech?

    A. In 8 minutes.

    B. In 10 minutes.

    C. In 27 minutes.

    D. On May 27th.

4. _____

Q：Who is this advertisement directed to?

    A. Employers.

    B. English teachers.

    C. Students who want to learn English.

    D. Trainers.

5. _____

Q：What should you do before answering questions on your test sheets?

    A. Use a pencil to write your name.

    B. Turn in your test sheets.

    C. Read the directions.

    D. Check your answers.

6. _____

Q：What are the passengers asked to do?

    A. Line up at the gate.

    B. Carry their own bags.

    C. Show their boarding pass.

    D. Go to the counter immediately.

7. _____

Q：What is the purpose of this announcement?

    A. To talk about traffic rules.

    B. To announce that schools and public officials are closed.

    C. To advise residents to conserve water.

    D. To ask residents to donate money to the victims of last night's flood.

8. _____

Q：What kind of job is advertised?

    A. Food handler.

    B. Secretary.

    C. English teacher.

    D. Personnel manager.

9. _____

Q：Who is the talk directed to?

    A. Teachers.

    B. Professors.

    C. Students.

    D. Newspaper office workers.

10. _____

Q：When will the heavy showers begin?

    A. Monday afternoon.

    B. Late tonight.

    C. Tomorrow morning.

    D. Sunday afternoon.

*短文獨白題一1-10題解答請見 253 頁。

● 短文獨白題二（一段對應三題）

　　短文獨白題二，設計的方式為一段式的談話，搭配三個問題。其中談話均由CD播出，題目的選項則會出現在試題本上，考生需閱讀後再做四個選項的選擇。題目以疑問詞（WH）的問句來問，也就是要考生能辨別時間，辨別地點，辨別原因，辨別人物以及辨別意圖等能力。此種題目的作答方式，一定要先看題目，題目有三題，所以對時間的掌握要更加注意。

◆ **聽力測驗試題11～40題，請聽CD完成以下10組30題模擬試題，並將答案寫在題號旁** 🎧 7-02 。

11. _____

Q：How can you make an appointment with Dr. Chad Smith?

    A. Press one.

    B. Press two.

    C. Stay on line.

    D. Wait for a beep.

12. _____

Q：What do you have to do if you have something urgent?

    A. Hang up the phone and call another phone number.

    B. Press one to speak with the assistance.

    C. Leave your message.

    D. Press two.

13. _____

Q：How can a caller leave a message?

    A. Call a cell phone number.

    B. Talk to the assistant.

    C. Wait for the beep.

    D. Make an appointment.

---

14. _____

Q：Which show will be first?

    A. Sport highlight.

    B. News.

    C. Weather report.

    D. An interview.

15. _____

Q：Who is the expert on finance management?

    A. Gina Wang.

    B. Brain Abrams.

    C. Jack Cook.

    D. the newscaster.

16. _____

Q：What is the show after the news?

    A. An interview.

    B. Sport highlight.

    C. Financial program.

    D. Weather forecast.

17. _____

Q：What is this announcement about?

    A. A vacation.

    B. A mail package.

    C. A walking tour.

    D. An economic situation.

18. _____

Q：What can NOT be found at the resort?

    A. A beach.

    B. A log cabin.

    C. A swimming pool.

    D. A tennis court.

19. _____

Q：Who might be interested in this ad?

    A. A retired worker who needs a health insurance.

    B. A construction worker who needs to train his body.

    C. An office worker who needs some relaxation.

    D. A homemaker who needs to buy some appliances.

20. _____

Q：Where does the announcement take place?

    A. At the parking garage.

    B. At the computer store.

    C. At the fair.

    D. At the symposium.

21. _____

Q：Who might be attending this event?

    A. Someone who is interested in high technology.

    B. Someone who seeks for some job offers.

    C. Someone who is interested in architecture.

    D. Someone who wants to improve their communication skill.

22. _____

Q：What will they do first?

    A. Look at some markets.

    B. Understand an outstanding group.

    C. Know about a new model.

    D. Listen to a speech.

----

23. _____

Q：Which number should a customer press to get more information?

    A. One.

    B. Two.

    C. Three.

    D. Four.

24. _____

Q：When are "NOT" the regular hours for this company?

    A. Monday at 7:00P.M.

    B. Saturday at 11:00A.M.

    C. Sunday at 7:00A.M.

    D. Tuesday at 5:00P.M.

25. _____

Q：What happens if a customer presses 5?

    A. The customer can track the order.

    B. The customer can order something.

    C. The customer can get the latest information about goods.

    D. The customer can hear the message again.

26. _____

Q：What is the purpose of the party?

    A. To review last year's performance.

    B. To honor the retirement of Ms. Rothman.

    C. To get a rest.

    D. To have a new fair.

27. _____

Q：Which adjective "CANNOT" describes Ms. Rothman?

    A. Accommodating.

    B. Industrious.

    C. Officious.

    D. Reliable.

28. _____

Q：What is Ms. Rothman going to do next?

    A. Take a trip.

    B. Have a baby.

    C. Give a speech.

    D. Complete her assignments.

---

29. _____

Q：Who is the talk directed to?

    A. Teachers.

    B. Patrons.

    C. Students.

    D. Office employees.

30. _____

Q：What's Professor Cruise's specialty?

    A. Economics.

    B. Research and development.

    C. Population.

    D. Politics.

31. _____

Q：Who is Dr. Thomas?

    A. A waiter.

    B. A teacher.

    C. An European politician.

    D. A bookstore owner.

---

32. _____

Q：Where is the speaker?

    A. On a plane.

    B. On a train.

    C. On a bus.

    D. On a ship.

33. _____

Q：Why should passengers stay in their seats?

    A. To keep safe from turbulence.

    B. To free the aisle.

    C. To watch the in-flight movie.

    D. To avoid the heavy air traffic.

34. _____

Q：How much time do they need before they take off?

    A. 25 minutes.

    B. 45 minutes.

    C. 35 minutes.

    D. It doesn't say.

35. _____

Q：What season is it?

    A. Spring.

    B. Summer.

    C. Autumn.

    D. Winter.

36. _____

Q：When will it rain?

    A. This afternoon.

    B. Tomorrow morning.

    C. Tomorrow evening.

    D. The day after tomorrow.

37. _____

Q：How many inches of snow are anticipated?

    A. 85.

    B. 12.

    C. 3.

    D. It doesn't say.

38. _____

Q：How much time you need if you take a regular train to the destination?

    A. 35 minutes.

    B. 55 minutes.

    C. 45 minutes.

    D. It doesn't say.

39. _____

Q：What is "NOT" provided on the train?

    A. Drinks.

    B. Snacks.

    C. Cigars.

    D. Coffee.

40.
_____

Q：In accordance with this announcement, who needs help as passengers
step off the train?

A. Physically challenged ones.

B. People at the age of 35.

C. Children under 12.

D. People who live in Bronx.

*短文獨白題二11-40題解答請見 260 頁。

■ 解答

◆ 短文獨白題—聽力測驗試題敘述內容與解答1～10題

1. Thanks for calling Office Helper hotline. We are here to serve you everyday from 9:00A.M to 5:00P.M. To place an order, please press 1. To hear our return policy, please press 2. To talk to our customer service, please stay on the line.

   （C）Q: What happens if a customer presses 2?

   　　A. The customer can talk to the customer service.

   　　B. The customer can order something.

   　　C. The customer can get information about return policy.

   　　D. The customer can get the money back.

2. Good evening, everybody, and welcome to the birthday party for John. As his supervisor, I am so happy to have this party for him. He is a nice coworker. OK, let's enjoy the party! And happy birthday to John.

   （A）Q: What is the relationship between the speaker and John?

   　　A. Manager and staff.

   　　B. Teacher and student.

   　　C. Parent and child.

   　　D. Husband and wife.

3. Attention, customers. In 10 minutes, author Sara Roberts is going to introduce her new book, "How to be rich". All interested please proceed to Room 8 now. Also, we would like to remind you again that we will be closed on May 27th. Have a nice day.

   （B）Q: When can people listen to a speech?

   　　A. In 8 minutes.

   　　B. In 10 minutes.

   　　C. In 27 minutes.

   　　D. On May 27th.

4. Is your language school looking to hire experienced English teachers? Do you want to hire teachers who have been trained with the latest methodology? Look no more. Graduates of the Global Teacher Training Institute are highly trained teachers able to teach your students very well. Come and hire one today!

(A) Q: Who is this advertisement directed to?

A. Employers.

B. English teachers.

C. Students who want to learn English.

D. Trainers.

5. When you get your test sheets, write your name in capital letters first. Read all the directions carefully before you try to answer each question. Please use pens, not pencils, to write your answers. When you finish your test, put your test sheets on your desk and then you can go home.

(C) Q: What should you do before answering questions on your test sheets?

A. Use a pencil to write your name.

B. Turn in your test sheets.

C. Read the directions.

D. Check your answers.

6. Flight 101 is now ready for boarding. All passengers please stand in line at the gate. If your carry-on bags are too large, please check them at the counter. Thanks for your cooperation.

(A) Q: What are the passengers asked to do?

A. Line up at the gate.

B. Carry their own bags.

C. Show their boarding pass.

D. Go to the counter immediately.

7. All schools and public office will be closed today due to last's night heavy rain. Some areas are flooded, so all residents are advised to stay home. Listen to the evening weather reports to find out tomorrow's school and public office schedule.

（B）Q: What is the purpose of this announcement?

    A. To talk about traffic rules.

    B. To announce that schools and public officials are closed.

    C. To advise residents to conserve water.

    D. To ask residents to donate money to the victims of last night's flood.

8. ABC Company is looking for a secretary. If you can speak English fluently, and have at least three years experience in a food industry, then we want you. Send your resume to our Personnel Office.

（B）Q: What kind of job is advertised?

    A. Food handler.

    B. Secretary.

    C. English teacher.

    D. Personnel manager.

9. Everyone, I am Professor Thomas. Welcome to this course. There will be two exams this term, and you will have to write three short papers. OK, let's start today's class.

（C）Q: Who is the talk directed to?

    A. Teachers.

    B. Professors.

    C. Students.

    D. Newspaper office workers.

10. I'm Charlie Lee with your weather forecast. There's a slight chance of rain this afternoon, possibly turning into heavy showers late tonight. There's an 80 percent chance of precipitation tomorrow morning, and temperatures will be colder than today.

(B) Q: When will the heavy showers begin?

      A. Monday afternoon.

      B. Late tonight.

      C. Tomorrow morning.

      D. Sunday afternoon.

◆ 短文獨白題─聽力測驗試題中文翻譯1～10題

1. 謝謝您來電協助熱線。我們每天早上九點到下午五點為您服務。若要訂貨，請按一。要聽退貨辦法，請按二。要和客服人員對談，請在線上稍候。

    Q：若顧客按二會有何情形？

        A. 顧客可以和客服人員對談。

        B. 顧客可以訂貨。

        C. 顧客可以獲得退貨資訊。

        D. 顧客可以將錢要回。

2. 大家晚安，歡迎各位來到約翰的生日派對。身為他的主管，我非常高興替他安排這場派對。他是一位很好的同事。好，讓我們好好享受這個派對吧！並祝福約翰生日快樂。

    Q：說話者與約翰的關係為何？

        A. 經理與員工。

        B. 老師與學生。

        C. 家長與小孩。

        D. 先生與太太。

3. 顧客們請注意。再十分鐘，作者莎拉羅勃茲將要介紹她的新書，「如何變富有」。所有有興趣者請現在前往第八會議室。同時，我們要再次提醒您，本店五月二十七日不營業。祝福大家愉快。

    Q：何時聽眾可以聽演講？

        A. 再過八分鐘。

        B. 再過十分鐘。

        C. 再過二十七分鐘。

        D. 五月二十七日。

4. 您的語文中心想僱用有經驗的英文老師嗎？您想要僱用經過

最新教學法訓練的老師嗎？您不用再找了。全球老師訓練機構的畢業生都是經過高度訓練的老師，能夠將您的學生教到盡善盡美。今天就來這裡僱用一位吧！

Q：本則廣告所要陳述的對象是誰？

A. 雇主。

B. 英文老師。

C. 想要學英文的學生。

D. 講師。

5. 拿到考卷時，先用大寫字母寫上名字。在回答每一題前，要先仔細地閱讀所有的規定。請使用原子筆，而不要使用鉛筆來回答問題。完成考試後，把考卷放在桌上，你便可以回家了。

Q：在回答考試卷上的問題前要先做什麼？

A. 用鉛筆寫你的名字。

B. 繳交考卷。

C. 閱讀規定。

D. 檢查答案。

6. 101號班機的乘客請準備登機。所有乘客請在登機門前排隊。假如您的手提行李過大，請交至櫃檯託運。感謝您的合作。

Q：乘客被要求做什麼？

A. 在登機門前排隊。

B. 拿自己的行李。

C. 出示登機證。

D. 立即至櫃檯處。

7. 由於昨晚的大雨，所有的學校與公家機關今天均停止上班上課。有些地區淹大水，所以建議所有居民都先待在家中。請聽晚間的氣象報告來掌握明日學校與公家機關上班上課的狀況。

Q：這項廣播的目的為何？

A. 討論交通規則。

B. 宣布學校與公家機關停班停課。

C. 建議居民儲水。

D. 要求居民捐錢給昨晚洪水的災民。

8.ABC公司正在找尋祕書。假如你能將英文說的流利，以及至少有三年在食品業的經驗，那我們就需要你。把履歷表寄至我們的人事部門。

　　Q：這是什麼工作需求的廣告？

　　A. 食物處理者。

　　B. 祕書。

　　C. 英文老師。

　　D. 人事部經理。

9.各位，我是湯瑪士教授。歡迎來到這門課。這學期會有兩次考試，你們也將交出三份的短篇報告。好的，讓我們開始今日的課程。

　　Q：這項談話是對誰說的？

　　A. 老師。

　　B. 教授。

　　C. 學生。

　　D. 報社的工作者。

10.我是李查理帶給各位氣象報導。今日下午有些微下雨的機會，稍晚可能會轉變為大雨。明日早上有百分之八十的降雨量，氣溫也會比今日更冷。

　　Q：大雨何時開始？

　　A. 週一下午。

　　B. 今晚稍晚。

　　C. 明早。

　　D. 週日下午。

◆短文獨白題二聽力測驗試題敘述內容與解答11～40題

1. Q11～13

You have reached the voice mail of Dr. Chad Smith's office. If this is an emergency, please hang up and call my cell phone number. If you want to make an appointment, please press one to speak with my assistant. If you want to ask some questions about prescriptions or medical advice, please press two. Otherwise, wait for the beep and leave your message. Thank you.

（A）11.How can you make an appointment with Dr. Chad Smith?

        A. Press one.

        B. Press two.

        C. Stay on line.

        D. Wait for a beep.

（A）12.What do you have to do if you have something urgent?

        A. Hang up the phone and call another phone number.

        B. Press one to speak with the assistance.

        C. Leave your message.

        D. Press two.

（C）13.How can a caller leave a message?

        A. Call a cell phone number.

        B. Talk to the assistant.

        C. Wait for the beep.

        D. Make an appointment.

2. Q14～16

Coming up after the news is our sports highlights. Then, our reporter Gina Wang will interview Brian Abrams about his new book, the best seller in the bookstores, "How to manage your finances and save a big money before 30." Mr. Abrams is a known professional on finance management. This is an educational and informative show, and you cannot miss it. Now, here's Jack Cook with today's news.

（B）14.Which show will be first?

       A. Sport highlight.

       B. News.

       C. Weather report.

       D. An interview.

（B）15.Who is the expert on finance management?

       A. Gina Wang.

       B. Brain Abrams.

       C. Jack Cook.

       D. The newscaster.

（B）16.What is the show after the news?

       A. An interview.

       B. Sport highlight.

       C. Financial program.

       D. Weather forecast.

3. Q17～19

Feel tired due to your daily hard work? Want to have a vacation and relax? We offer weekend and weeklong packages just as you want!

Stay at a resort, and enjoy our two swimming pools, four tennis courts and a private sandy beach. You will love our luxury accommodations and economical prices. Call today to book your tour, and you'll be ready for your beautiful vacation.

（A）17.What is this announcement about?

      A. A vacation.

      B. A mail package.

      C. A walking tour.

      D. An economic situation.

（B）18.What can NOT be found at the resort?

      A. A beach.

      B. A log cabin.

      C. A swimming pool.

      D. A tennis court.

（C）19.Who might be interested in this ad?

      A. A retired worker who needs a health insurance.

      B. A construction worker who needs to train his body.

      C. An office worker who needs some relaxation.

      D. A homemaker who needs to buy some appliances.

4. Q20～22

Ladies and gentlemen: it is my honor to welcome such an outstanding group of foreign buyers to the opening of our Computer Fair. As you all know, this is the largest trade exhibition in the nation, and I am sure your presence at this trade event will be crucial to its success. More importantly, your participation will lead to a better understanding of the market opportunities here in our field. Thank you for your attention. And now, let's have a look at this advanced new model.

（C）20.Where does the announcement take place?

      A. At the parking garage.

      B. At the computer store.

C. At the fair.

D. At the symposium.

（A）21.Who might be attending this event?

A. Someone who is interested in high technology.

B. Someone who seeks for some job offers.

C. Someone who is interested in architecture.

D. Someone who wants to improve their communication skill.

（C）22. What will they do first?

A. Look at some markets.

B. Understand an outstanding group.

C. Know about a new model.

D. Listen to a speech.

5. Q23～25

Thanks for calling the Building Your Home hotline. We are here to serve you from Monday to Friday between the hours of 8:00A.M. and 8:00P.M., weekend between the hours of 8:00A.M. and 12:00P.M.. If you are calling at a different time, please call back during our regular hours. To place an order, please press 1. To track the order you placed before, please press 2. To hear our return policy, please press 3. To have the latest information about our commodities, please press 4. To repeat the menu, please press 5. Building Your Home is proud to announce its annual sale starts next Monday. All goods will be marked down 40%. Take advantage of this amazing sale, so place more orders and save.

（D）23.Which number should a customer press to get more information?

A. One.

B. Two.

C. Three.

D. Four.

(C) 24. When are "NOT" the regular hours for this company?

    A. Monday at 7:00P.M.

    B. Saturday at 11:00A.M.

    C. Sunday at 7:00A.M.

    D. Tuesday at 5:00P.M.

(D) 25. What happens if a customer presses 5?

    A. The customer can track the order.

    B. The customer can order something.

    C. The customer can get the latest information about goods.

    D. The customer can hear the message again.

6. Q26～28

Good evening, everybody, and welcome to the farewell party for Mary Rothman. Even though you hear enough from me all the time, I'd like to get in a few words for a few minutes before the party begins. Mary has worked for our company for the past 30 years. As her supervisor, I can always closely observe her performance. She is a reliable and hardworking individual, and always completes her assignments in a timely and accurate manner. Thanks to her friendly manner and cooperative and accommodating spirit, she is certainly a pleasure to work with. I think we will miss her after her retirement. We know she will get a well-deserved rest during her upcoming cruise to Africa. Bon voyage, my dear Mary!

(B) 26. What is the purpose of the party?

    A. To review last year's performance.

    B. To honor the retirement of Ms. Rothman.

C. To get a rest.

D. To have a new fair.

（C）27. Which adjective "CANNOT" describe Ms. Rothman?

    A. Accommodating.

    B. Industrious.

    C. Officious.

    D. Reliable.

（A）28. What is Ms. Rothman going to do next?

    A. Take a trip.

    B. Have a baby.

    C. Give a speech.

    D. Complete her assignments.

7. Q29～31

Good morning, everyone. I am Professor Cruise. Welcome to this course-Introduction to Politics. All of you may hear that I am an easygoing teacher and seldom give students tests, but let me remind you that things are going to change. There will be four exams this term, in addition to which you will have to write 7 short research papers. You can get your textbooks at the school bookstore. Buy paperbacks although their prices are still a little steep. OK, if you don't have further questions, let's start for the day. And remember that next week we'll have a special guest, Dr. Thomas, the author of several best-sellers about politics, and he will give us a presentation about his latest research on European politics.

（C）29.Who is the talk directed to?

    A. Teachers.

    B. Patrons.

C. Students.

D. Office employees.

(D) 30. What's Professor Cruise's specialty?

A. Economics.

B. Research and development.

C. Population.

D. Politics.

(B) 31. Who is Dr. Thomas?

A. A waiter.

B. A writer.

C. An European politician.

D. A bookstore owner.

8. Q32~34

Trans-Pacific Air welcomes you aboard its nonstop service from New York to Paris. We are presently experiencing a delay because of the heavy air traffic. It will be close to 45 minutes before our takeoff. Please accept our humble apology. The captain has asked us to serve complimentary beverages and snacks to make the wait less uncomfortable. You may unbuckle your seat belts now, however, in order that we can serve you drinks much more easily, please remain seated. Also, our in-flight movie will start in 25 minutes after we take off. If your need any assistance, please ask our flight attendants for help. Thank you for your cooperation, and enjoy the trip.

(A) 32. Where is the speaker?

A. On a plane.

B. On a train.

C. On a bus.

D. On a ship.

（B）33.Why should passengers stay in their seats?

    A. To keep safe from turbulence.

    B. To free the aisle.

    C. To watch the in-flight movie.

    D. To avoid the heavy air traffic.

（B）34.How much time do they need before they take off?

    A. 25 minutes.

    B. 45 minutes.

    C. 35 minutes.

    D. It doesn't say.

9. Q35～37

I am Susan Jackson with your three-day weather forecast. After a spell of hot weather, a cold front will push into the region by late afternoon. There's an 85 percent chance of precipitation tomorrow morning, turning into snowstorm or hailstorm by evening. Over 12 inches of snow are expected to fall before the storm moves out of the region the day after tomorrow. Since this weather isn't typical for a cool fall day, perhaps we should pay more attention to these changes in weather. Now, let's go back to Sara Roberts with today's international news.

（C）35.What season is it?

    A. Spring.

    B. Summer.

    C. Autumn.

    D. Winter.

（B）36.When will it rain?

      A. This afternoon.

      B. Tomorrow morning.

      C. Tomorrow evening.

      D. The day after tomorrow.

（B）37.How many inches of snow are anticipated?

      A. 85.

      B. 12.

      C. 3.

      D. It doesn't say.

10. Q38～40

Welcome all passengers. This is the express train to the Bronx. The non-stop trip takes around 35 minutes. If you are looking for the regular train, which takes approximately 55 minutes to the Bronx, please walk across the platform to Track T immediately. Also, let me remind you that this is a non-smoking train, so any kind of smoking is definitely not allowed. And please be informed that we offer cheap snacks and refreshments here, you can ask attendants if you need some. As you step off the express train, please assist elderly and handicapped travelers and watch for the steps. Thank you for your kind cooperation, Next stop, the Bronx!

（B）38.How much time do you need if you take a regular train to the destination?

      A. 35 minutes.

      B. 55 minutes.

      C. 45 minutes.

      D. It doesn't say.

（C）39.What is "NOT" provided on the train?

      A. Drinks.

      B. Snacks.

      C. Cigars.

      D. Coffee.

（A）40.In accordance with this announcement, who needs help as passengers step off the train?

      A. Physically challenged ones.

      B. People at the age of 35.

      C. Children under 12.

      D. People who live in Bronx.

◆ 短文獨白題二聽力測驗試題中文翻譯11～40題

1.

您已經撥到查德史密斯醫生診所的電話答錄。假如這是緊急事件，請掛掉改播我的手機號碼。假如你想要預約，請按一和我的助理聯繫。如果你想要問有關於處方與醫藥方面的意見，請按二。否則，請等待嗶一聲再留下你的訊息。謝謝。

11. 你如何能與查德史密斯醫生約診？
    A. 按一。
    B. 按二。
    C. 保持在線上。
    D. 等待嗶一聲。

12. 如果你有緊急事件，應該如何做？
    A. 掛掉電話播另一支電話號碼。
    B. 按一與助理通話。
    C. 留言。
    D. 按二。

13. 來電者如何留訊息？
    A. 打手機號碼。
    B. 與助理談。
    C. 等待嗶一聲。
    D. 預約。

2.

新聞過後是我們的重點體育消息。然後我們的記者吉娜王將會訪問布萊恩艾柏斯有關於他的新書，一本暢銷書「如何在三十歲前管理你的財務並存下大錢」。艾柏斯先生是一位有名的財務管理專家。這是一場有教育性與知識性的節目，你絕不能錯

過。現在，先由傑克庫克先帶來今日新聞。

14. 哪一個節目先進行？
    A. 體育消息。
    B. 新聞。
    C. 氣象報導。
    D. 訪問。

15. 誰是財務管理專家？
    A. 吉娜王。
    B. 布萊恩艾柏斯。
    C. 傑克庫克。
    D. 主播。

16. 哪一個節目在新聞過後？
    A. 訪問。
    B. 體育消息。
    C. 財務節目。
    D. 氣象報導。

3.
因為你每日辛勤的工作而感到疲累嗎？想要有一個假期來放鬆嗎？我們提供你要的週末與週間的套裝行程。待在度假村，享受我們的兩個游泳池，四個網球場，與一個私人的沙灘。你會愛上我們豪華的住宿與經濟的價格。今天就打電話來訂你的旅程，你已經準備好你的美麗的假期了！

17. 這個敘述是有關？
    A. 一個假期。
    B. 一個郵件包裹。

C. 一個步行的行程。

D. 一個經濟情勢。

18. 在度假村中哪一項無法找到？

    A. 海灘。

    B. 小木屋。

    C. 泳池。

    D. 網球場。

19. 誰可能會對這則廣告有興趣？

    A. 一位想要健保的退休員工。

    B. 一位想訓練身體的建築工人。

    C. 一位想要放鬆的上班族。

    D. 一位需要買家電用品的家庭主婦。

4.

各位女士先生：這是我的榮幸來歡迎這群傑出的外國買家來到我們的先進電腦展開幕。如同各位所知道，這是本國最大的貿易展，而我相信你們的出現對於這展覽的成功有極大的重要性。更重要的是，你的參與將導致對我們的這個領域的市場機會有更進一步深入的了解。謝謝你的注意，現在請先來看看這個最先進的新機型。

20. 這項廣播是在何處播放？

    A. 停車場。

    B. 電腦商店。

    C. 展示會。

    D. 研討會。

21. 誰會有興趣參與這活動？

A. 對高科技有興趣的人。

B. 想找工作的人。

C. 對建築有興趣的人。

D. 對想要改善溝通技巧有興趣的人。

22. 他們將先做什麼？

A. 看一些市場。

B. 了解傑出的一群人。

C. 了解新機型。

D. 聽演說。

5.

感謝你來電「建立你的家」熱線。我們在這裡為你服務，從週一到週五早上八點到晚上八點，週末是早上八點到中午十二點，如果你是非營業時間來電，請在我們營業的時間再來電。要下訂單，請按一。要查詢之前的訂單，請按二。要聽我們的退貨政策，請按三。要聽我們最新商品的資訊，請按四。要重複聆聽，請按五。建立你的家很驕傲的要告知你我們的年度銷售下週一要開始了，所有的商品會降價到六折。利用這次驚人的超低價，要多訂多省錢喔！

23. 若要更多的資訊要按幾？

A. 一。

B. 二。

C. 三。

D. 四。

24. 以下哪個時間不是一般營業時間？

A. 週一晚七點。

B. 週六早十一點。

C. 週日早七點。

D. 週二午五點。

25. 假如顧客按五會發生什麼事？

    A. 顧客可查詢訂貨。

    B. 顧客可訂貨。

    C. 顧客可得到最新商品的資訊。

    D. 顧客可再聽到訊息一遍。

6.

大家晚安。歡迎來到瑪麗茹斯曼的歡送會。雖然你們平常總是聽夠我所說的話，但我在派對開始之前還是想說幾句話。瑪麗已經在我們公司上班三十年了。我身為她的主管，我可以每日近距離的觀察她的工作表現。她是一位可靠認真的工作者，總是準時且精確地完成她的工作任務。由於她的友善態度與合作與包容力強的精神，她的確是個可以與她愉快工作的對象。我想我們在她退休後將會很想念她的。我們知道她將會得到應得的休息，在她即將去非洲的這趟航程中。一路順風，親愛的瑪麗！

26. 這個派對的目的是？

    A. 檢視去年的績效。

    B. 榮耀茹斯曼女士的退休。

    C. 得到休息。

    D. 辦新展示會。

27. 下列哪一個形容詞無法描述茹斯曼女士？

    A. 隨和的。

    B. 勤奮的。

    C. 愛管閒事的。

    D. 可靠的。

28. 茹斯曼女士下一步將要做什麼？

    A. 旅行。

    B. 生小孩。

    C. 演說。

    D. 完成她的工作任務。

7.

大家早，我是克魯斯教授。歡迎來到這堂政治學導論的課程。你們所有人可能有聽過我是一位很隨和的老師，而且很少給學生考試。但是讓我提醒各位，情況可能不一樣了。這學期將會有四回的考試，此外還必須寫七份的短篇報告。你們可以在學校書局買到教科書。要買平裝本，雖然它們的價格仍有些高。好的，假如沒有任何問題，我們就開始今日的課程。同時也記得下週我們將有一個特別的演講貴賓，湯瑪士博士，他是有關政治類暢銷書的作者，他會帶來他最新有關於歐洲政治研究的演說。

29. 這段對話是對誰說的？

    A. 老師。

    B. 顧客。

    C. 學生。

    D. 辦公室員工。

30. 克魯斯教授的專業是？

    A. 經濟學。

    B. 研發。

    C. 人口。

    D. 政治學。

31. 誰是湯瑪士博士？

A. 服務生。
B. 作者。
C. 歐洲的政治人士。
D. 書店老闆。

8.
泛太平洋航空公司歡迎你搭乘這趟從紐約到巴黎的直飛行程。由於空中交通繁忙，我們目前正面臨延誤的情況。大約再四十五分鐘我們才會起飛。請接受我們誠懇的歉意。機長已經要求我們提供免費的飲料與點心來讓等待變得輕鬆一些。現在你可以解開你的安全帶，但是為了讓我們服務您飲料更方便些，所以請待在原位上。機上的電影將在起飛後二十五分放映。如果你需要任何協助，請找我們的空服員。謝謝你的合作，並享受你的這趟旅程。

32. 說話者人位於何處？
    A. 飛機上。
    B. 火車上。
    C. 公車上。
    D. 船上。

33. 為何乘客應該待在他們的座位上？
    A. 因為亂流而要保持安全。
    B. 讓出走道。
    C. 看機上的電影。
    D. 避免繁忙的空中交通。

34. 他們還需要多少時間才能起飛？
    A. 二十五分鐘。
    B. 四十五分鐘。

C. 三十五分鐘。

D. 沒有提到。

9.

我是蘇珊傑克森帶給各位三天的氣象報導。在一陣子的熱天氣之後，午後稍晚將有一道冷鋒推進這個區域。明天早上會有百分之八十五的降雨量，到了晚上更轉為暴風雪或大冰雹。在暴風雪離開境內之前，到了後天預期會有超過十二英吋的積雪。由於這天氣不是典型的涼爽秋季，也許我們應更注意這些天氣的變化。現在先由莎拉羅勃茲帶來今日的國際新聞。

35. 現在的季節是？

A. 春。

B. 夏。

C. 秋。

D. 冬。

36. 何時將會下雨？

A. 今天下午。

B. 明天早上。

C. 明天晚上。

D. 後天。

37. 預期有多少吋的積雪？

A. 八十五。

B. 十二。

C. 三。

D. 文中未說明。

10.

歡迎各位乘客。這是到柏朗尼克斯的特快車。這趟無中途停靠的行程約要三十五分鐘。假如您找的是一般的列車，大約要五十五分鐘到柏朗尼克斯，請立刻到對面月臺的T軌道。同時讓我提醒你這是一趟非吸菸的火車，所以任何形式的吸菸都是絕對不被許可的。同時告知您我們在這裡提供便宜的點心與飲料，如果需要請洽服務人員。當你下離列車時，請協助老人與殘障旅客，並小心階梯。謝謝您的合作。下一站，柏朗尼克斯！

38. 假如搭乘普通的列車，到目的地要多少時間？
   A. 三十五分鐘。
   B. 五十五分鐘。
   C. 四十五分鐘。
   D. 文中未提及。

39. 火車上「沒有」提供什麼？
   A. 飲料。
   B. 點心。
   C. 雪茄。
   D. 咖啡。

40. 根據這個廣播，誰在下火車時需要幫助？
   A. 身體殘障人士。
   B. 年齡超過三十五歲者。
   C. 小於十二歲的小孩。
   D. 住在柏朗尼克斯的人。

筆記頁

筆記頁

筆記頁

國家圖書館出版品預行編目資料

全方位英文聽力速成／陳頎著.--初版.--臺北
市：書泉,2014.09
　面；　公分
ISBN 978-986-121-944-8（平裝附光碟片）
1.英語　2.讀本
805.18　　　　　　　　103014920

3AC8

全方位英文聽力速成

作　　者 ― 陳　頎(246.8)

發 行 人 ― 楊榮川

總 編 輯 ― 王翠華

主　　編 ― 朱曉蘋

責任編輯 ― 吳雨潔

封面設計 ― 吳佳臻

出 版 者 ― 書泉出版社

地　　址：106台北市大安區和平東路二段339號4樓

電　　話：(02)2705-5066　　傳　真：(02)2706-6100

網　　址：http://www.wunan.com.tw

電子郵件：shuchuan@shuchuan.com.tw

劃撥帳號：0 1 3 0 3 8 5 3

戶　　名：書泉出版社

經 銷 商：朝日文化

進退貨地址：新北市中和區橋安街15巷1號7樓

TEL：(02)2249-7714　　FAX：(02)2249-8715

法律顧問　林勝安律師事務所　林勝安律師

出版日期　2014年9月初版一刷

定　　價　新臺幣380元